And Both Shall Row

Also by Beth Lordan

August Heat

And Both Shall Row

A Novella and Stories

Beth Lordan

Picador USA
New York

Picador® USA is a registered trademark and is used by St. Martin's
Press under license from Pan Books Limited.

"The Widow" first appeared in *The Atlantic Monthly*, August 1987.
"The Cow Story" first appeared in *The Georgetown Review*, Spring 1993.
"The Dummy" first appeared in *The Atlantic Monthly*, August 1996.
"Running Out" first appeared in *The Atlantic Monthly*, May 1986.
"The Snake" first appeared in *The Gettysburg Review*, Summer 1997.
"Old Clayborne Trail" first appeared in *Farmer's Market*, Spring/Summer
1995.

Design by Ellen R. Sasahara

Library of Congress Cataloging-in-Publication Data

Lordan, Beth.
    And both shall row : a novella and stories / Beth Lordan.
        p.   cm.
    Contents: The widow—The cow story—The dummy—
        Running out—The snake—Old Clayborne Trail—And
    both shall row.
    ISBN 0-312-18682-7
    I. Title.
  PS3562.O73A53   1998
  813'.54—dc21   98-15745
                                                    CIP

First Picador USA Edition: August 1998

10 9 8 7 6 5 4 3 2 1

For
Lamar Herrin, Mike Curtis, and Walt Slatoff,
gamblers and guides

Contents

Acknowledgments

THE AUTHOR wishes to acknowledge the generous support of the New York State Council on the Arts, the National Endowment for the Arts, and the Illinois Arts Council during the writing of these stories.

And Both Shall Row

The Widow

THE MORNING WARREN BOYD dropped dead in his kitchen, he was the only living person on the farm. Just back of the barn two milk cows stood near each other in the light sun, staring across a small pasture toward three old apple trees. Farther off twelve heifers were working their way from a mud patch by a salt block down to a rock pile where blackberries were in bloom; they'd get to the shade of the willows about noon. The one that was mostly white, with an Africa-shaped black spot covering her left shoulder, took off running and bucking, but none of the others joined in, and so she calmed down and went back to grazing. The barn was empty. Up behind the vegetable garden a solitary lamb dozed under broad burdocks; near the back porch three laying hens murmured over small insects they found deep in the grass. The lilacs were gone by, and bees worked flowering weeds that had strayed from the first meadow into the yard. Unless one of the heifers took it into her mind to find her way out of the big pasture and into the road, or into some neighbor's garden, nobody would call Warren Boyd on the telephone and then come by to find out he was dead.

Warren's wife hovered, watching, in the upstairs bedroom, in her brown-flowered flannel nightgown, with her ankles long beneath her. Her name was Ann, and she'd been dead three years.

Giving up life had been harder for Ann than for Warren, who just walked into the broken square of sunlight in front of the sink and fell without thinking about it. She had let life go at last only because she understood, suddenly, that once she was dead she'd have time to devote herself to the study of Warren. She had devoted her efforts and attention to him for forty-two years, except for the few years when their daughter, Susan, was alive. But much of that time was spent just living—cooking, of course, and chores, and seeing other people, and peculiar things like Susan dying, with all that surprise and grief; and then giving attention to seasons and weather, deciding things and choosing between, arranging pillows so that she could fall asleep, sleeping itself, growing old. Her life had seemed endless and perverse, designed to keep her from the work of finding Warren out, which was what she had wanted to do since the first time she saw him in his splendor.

So when she was dying, seventy-one years old and rebellious, in the hospital in Livingston, she had suddenly understood that the three wishes everyone talked about their whole lives were given out at the moment of death. She had felt again the beginnings of the great excitement that had come over her the first time she saw Warren Boyd transformed, the excitement that all that living had kept putting aside.

That first time, they'd been married about a year, and she knew Warren some, knew he was fussy about his eggs but would never complain, knew he would always sleep on the side away from the wall, however she arranged the bedroom, knew how his hair grew on the back of his neck, and that he got corns on his left foot but not on his right. They had come quickly to habits of living together. Every morning, in the dead dark of winter or the paler dark of summer, she shut off the alarm and got up; if she was feeling tender, she'd take care not to let a draft come under the covers and chill him. Downstairs she'd put on the coffee and call once, "Warren!" back up the stairwell. By the time his breakfast was ready, he'd be there, dressed but not shaved, and neither of them talked over breakfast. He'd eat and go out to milk, and she'd dress in the bathroom off the kitchen while the dishes soaked in hot soapy water in the round white dish-pan. Then she'd do them up, start the baking, water the ferns in the dim parlor, and go back up to the bedroom to make the bed and open the curtains. She hated to be done with the upstairs work before he came back from the barn; she liked best to be just beginning the bed when the screen door slammed as he came in. That way, by the time he finished shaving downstairs, she was in the kitchen getting ready to go out to the garden, or making a list of something, or sorting through something, and she could feel as busy and as inattentive to him as he always seemed in the mornings to her. Most mornings she'd gather up yesterday's dirty clothes and put them in the hamper, straighten the dresser tops, check that the clothes in the drawers were neat, run the dust mop under the bed, and shake the throw rug out the window three crisp snaps; then she'd go and stand at the window and watch for him to come out of the milk house before she finished the bed. She had once explained to herself, early in her marriage, that those minutes with the window open and the bed-clothes turned back aired the bedding; she never doubted it again.

One early summer morning she stood by the window with the blue striped throw rug in her hand and the smell of ripe hay just reaching her from down below. She was thinking about jelly, for no particular reason, about steaming jelly dripping slowly through the pudding bag into a big glass bowl, when she saw her husband come out of the cool gloom of the milk-house doorway into the deep shadow cast by the barn. He walked as if he were under water, slowly and gracefully, his hands lifting slightly at every movement, every step unnaturally high and delicate. In every fold of his gray work clothes, in the hair on his head, and among the bristles of his unshaven face clung tiny air bubbles, gleaming like glass pearls. He stepped carefully to the edge of the shadow and stopped, a small smile sweet across his face as he turned his head slowly to look back at the barn, the bubbles shimmering in every shadow of his person there in the cool shade.

Ann stared, struck thoughtless by this vision of her young husband suddenly submerged. She scarcely breathed, feeling something like deep memory, and nearly cried out in rage when he stepped, at last, from the shadow onto the sunlit lawn, and his bubbles disappeared as his foot came down hard and ordinary in the light.

She was still at the window, holding the rug with both hands tight under her chin, when he called up the stairs, "Ann?" She didn't answer, though she tensed with dread that he might come up. "Ann? I'm going to Jim's; you need just tea and salt?" he called, still from the foot of the stairs. From the blackboard, she thought, he knows it from the blackboard, fighting to recover the ordinary. "Ann?"

She could hear in his voice that he meant to come up, so she shouted back, angry and loud, "Yes!"

"Okay," he said. As she heard him go down the back steps, she went to the unmade bed, and lay down, and covered her chest with the rug.

She never expected to see such a thing again. That night, and for a few nights after, she went to bed early to avoid him. But time passed, haying came and passed, and the vision faded. She was eager to have it go, to fill its place again with the real Warren, his silences and his digestion, his pleasure at jokes he brought from Jim's store, his responsible worry over crops and equipment. They bought three more heifers that year, and the next farm went up for sale at a price they couldn't meet. In the spring they burned down the old pig shed and doubled their garden space; just after Christmas, Susan was born. Those were good, ordinary years—Ann thought so then, and her memory always held that time as wholesome, sturdy, and serious.

And then one night, when Susan was five and the summer night was loud and calm and Ann lay in bed alone, almost drowsing beneath the sheet, she heard the screen door slam and not slam again. A thought of Warren sitting on the back step in the dark came into Ann's mind, and with it came the thought of sitting quietly beside him in her nightdress in the night air. She got up and went to the window; from there she could see if a light was on in the barn, or if cigarette smoke came from near the back door, invisible below her. No light in the barn, no sign or smell of smoke from below. Ann leaned within the drifting curtain, unalarmed, looking out over the quiet yard to the swarm of slow lightning bugs rising in the apple tree. A rectangle of light from the kitchen window lay across the short grass she had mowed that morning. The grass in the light seemed bleached. Ann thought of frost, of Susan's red boot toe breaking iced puddles in the barnyard as she jumped down from the back of the truck where Warren had let her ride with the Christmas tree. Ann smiled, and then she saw Warren, over near the small shed where the lambs slept.

The shed was a heavy form in the dark, skirted and ruffled with the lighter shadows of burdocks, and in the dense dark the ground was black. Nearby, Susan's sandpile was only a lightening of the darkness, but Warren was bright, his hair clearly brown, with bits of gray showing like kernels of rice; his eyes were blue, and the clean undershirt he had put on after milking was as white as if it hung on the line in clear sunlight. He stood with his hands high in the air, showing the darker dampness under his arms, and then he did a somersault on the black grass, his jeans a blur of faded denim coming down from the dark to the dark. Warren somersaulted again and then again, toward the window light and the door light laid like cloths on the grass.

Ann dropped to her knees as he tumbled, and all she knew was his brown and white and blue in the uncolored dark. She was triumphant and breathless as he came, revealed, through the dark. She saw him roll toward and then into the spread house light, and his colors bleached in the yellow light, and his last roll landed him standing, drained and appropriate, near the back step.

She knelt by the window a moment, and then a moment more, and she began to plan as her breath returned and her joints reclaimed themselves. Through the screen came the sound and then the smell

5

of a cigarette lit below. Ann stood and turned; she went down the stairs and across the cool kitchen floor to the back door.

Warren sat on the step, his undershirt yellow in the light, his smoke hanging in the still air. She pushed open the screen door and he turned his head to her. She stepped out and let the door bang shut, and sat down where he shifted to make room for her.

"I heard you come out," she explained, and she put her hand almost shyly on his rounded back.

"Hot," he said, and nodded, smoking, looking off into the dark.

His back was dry. No blade of grass, no leaf of clover, no small twig or crushed insect, no proof that he had done what she had seen him do. She watched the fireflies in the dark and heard the moths' quick small thuds on the screen, and she sighed. He drew again on the cigarette and snapped the butt in a long arch to the driveway. She smoothed her thin nightdress over her knees. That was the second time.

All summer Ann kept watch; she and Susan passed the days with kerchiefs tied over their hair against the fumbling accidental landings of June bugs. The garden flourished as never before, and hay prices dropped. Early evenings Warren would finish the milking and take Susan up to the pond in the west pasture to swim; she'd fall asleep beside him on the drive back down, and Ann would come out to carry her in from the truck. Jim sold his store to a stranger named Frenchie and moved south; Warren killed a laying hen by mistake in September, and Ann pulled five leathery eggs from the body as Susan counted them, checking her facts for show-and-tell. Ann made apple butter, and some rainy evenings all three of them would play dominoes, keeping score on the back of an envelope.

But Ann watched Warren all that winter without another miracle, and all that spring. In the summer Susan caught a cold, and the cold went to her chest; in early August they took her to the hospital. She accepted the shots and oxygen tent and the meals on trays as she had accepted the rest of her life, but in the last week of August she died.

Warren and Ann, numbed and terrified by the simplicity of Susan's death, were quiet and separate all through the winter, and Ann closed herself against the watching. The house was silent with their unshared grief. In the spring they sold half the hatch of chicks, leaving unmentioned their memory of Susan's enchantment with them. Jim came back from the South and set up a small diner in town, where Warren often drank coffee midmornings with other farmers and the Baptist minister and anyone else who came in, while Ann dusted and polished and stayed indoors, away from the windows, even though the weather was fine and the chickens ran wild up and down the yard. A stranger bought the old Clayborne Inn and converted it to apartments, though he kept the hotel bar open. In the fall, one night after everything else was done, Warren and Ann sat in the silent living room, Ann hemming curtains and Warren holding the paper unread on his lap. Warren sighed and got up and got his gray cap from the kitchen.

"I'm going into town for a while," he said.

She nodded and kept sewing. She heard the truck start and pause at the end of the driveway, and then roll off down the road for Clayborne. She worked on until midnight. Then she bit her thread and folded the flowered cloth neatly into the box beside her chair, went into the kitchen and turned off the backyard light, and went on up the stairs to bed.

Hours later a sudden silence woke her. She heard rain, and maybe thunder, before she felt that Warren was not in bed. She went to the window and saw the truck parked in the usual place. She went downstairs. The doors were still locked, and Warren was not there. She cupped her hands beside her eyes to look out the kitchen window.

Through the dark and the steady light rain she saw Warren push open the door of the truck cab. He stepped out and down, paused before he swung the door shut, paused again with his hand against the truck. "Why, he's drunk!" Ann thought, astounded at this new possibility, after all these years—a Warren who would drink more than a single bottle of beer. He stood there and lifted both hands to his face as if he had just awakened. He ran his hands up over his cheeks and eyes and forehead and pushed his gray cap back so far it fell off and landed behind him on the truck step.

Warren smiled and turned his head to look where the hat had gone. Then he straightened. He looked at the house, and, as he turned his arms in a low shrug, a soft brilliance rose from him. Like mist off a barn roof, something curled from the surfaces of Warren, from his hatless head and his open barn jacket, from the thick palms of his hands. He raised his hands slowly higher, and the mist around him flickered in pale colors. He turned a full slow circle on the gravel, his arms out, the bright, thin color trailing about him like veils in the rain. His face was wet. He stood for a long moment, with his arms lifted wide and the pale mist licking around him, and then he turned again, bent carefully for his cap, and stood, extinguished in the light of a cloudy dawn. He adjusted the gray cap carefully, and walked off to the barn. That was the third time, and Ann began to understand, though she didn't think of it as love, and she began again to watch.

For the rest of their lives together, between the buying and selling and choosing and changing, as they again found ways of living together that were easy and pleasant, she kept watch. Warren was transformed for her again and again, but never completely, never sufficiently. As the duties of living centered more and more on the needs of her own body and his, she grew frustrated with the solitude of her vigil, but she had always known that nothing she could ask or admit would help her discover whether he knew of his splendor, or whether he took care to hide or display it.

So when the three wishes came to her, as she lay with her gray hair flattened against her head in that hospital bed, Ann chose to remain with Warren until his death. She clearly understood her intentions: without breathing or sleeping or pain or work, she would spend her time at the windows, and she would watch Warren without pause. And if nothing changed, if the splendors came and faded in the now familiar and unsatisfying way even as she watched so steadily, perhaps at the moment of *his* death she would be able to see or discover what that splendor had been, what he had meant by it.

In those three years she saw Warren mysterious a few more times, and she saw and heard other things. She watched him come up from the barn early on autumn mornings, through the area leached of color by the strong floodlight, and she saw, as she had not before, his reluctance in that empty space, how he walked with his head doggedly lowered as if he would stop forever in the emptiness if he dared see it. She heard him, evenings, moving uncertainly, like a broken habit, down in the kitchen; she learned of his secret love for pork chops, and the smell of the frying chops came to signal suppertime as the dishwater smell of boiling potatoes once had. She traced the visions through her memory, trying to find the pattern. She learned to notice his hats; he wore the red Agway cap only to the barn and his own fields, the stained white Sherwin-Williams Paint cap whenever he meant to hammer or saw, and the plain gray cap for town and when he was sad. She learned that she would see the visions only when he went hatless. The hats were her only firm discovery about the mystery in all three years of waiting by the windows, and so by the morning Warren died, she was glad—glad to be at the moment of her greatest opportunity.

Ann heard him fall, and she waited upstairs until she was certain that the silence in the kitchen was utter and final before she went down. Warren lay on his side in front of the sink, with his left arm stretched out and pointing toward the kitchen table, where the *Weekly Shopper* lay open. His red Agway cap was firmly on his head, and Ann could see the gray hairs spiking out the opening in the back. The sunshine was bright across his gray-shirted shoulders. Ann knelt down beside him. Outside, the chickens kept up a steady muttering that hid the sound of the mowing machine up in the field that Warren had sold the year before to Jim's son.

Ann waited and waited, and the patch of sunlight on the kitchen floor began to shrink. Finally she became afraid, and sat back against the cupboards under the sink, and pulled her knees up to her chest. She watched: in a summer suddenness the kitchen grew dim. Ann knew he had taken his first wish and was gone, without even knowing she was there.

The two milk cows were moaning out by the barn, and the chickens had gone into the shed as the evening began to come down. Ann lowered her face to her knees, but she stayed by the cupboards, hugging her shins, her knees tight to her chest. The telephone began to ring in the living room. Ann waited. The telephone stopped.

Ann sat the whole night there on the kitchen floor, bearing the knowledge that he had gone. She had never imagined such a weight; it settled over and through her, a dark cold.

In the morning Jim's son knocked at the kitchen door and peered through the screen at Warren's body there by the table. He peered and went away, and Ann lifted her face from her knees. She rocked a little, watching Warren's stillness. Well, she thought, and let a ripple of bitter disappointment rise through her, felt the emptiness flow in like light behind it. Well, she thought again. Carefully she let down her arms, released her thin legs, and rose.

She stepped past him and started back upstairs, as if she had work to do. Over the third step, just where the stairs turned, she remembered how Warren had shimmered that first time, and as she stopped, the sweet red smell of raspberries came to her, and she could almost feel the steam from the cooking jelly rising into her face. She went on up to the bedroom and stood among the curtains at the open window, and made her second wish, for tears.

The Cow Story

FOR REASONS SHE perhaps knew, the nameless cow belonging to Byron Doatze chose the afternoon of the only tornado in Clayborne's history for her great escapade. She seemed at first not to notice that she was outside the makeshift fencing. She moved slowly, grazing; when she reached far back under the fence for a bite from her own pasture, the skin of her old throat stretched and trembled.

She wandered along the fence and then crossed Byron's dirt driveway, sampled the lawn, and took a slow look at his house. After a good while she got to the road. She had lived her entire unbred and leisured life on the one acre Byron had kept when he came back and sold off his father's farm, so she shouldn't have felt that first step onto smooth macadam as an invitation to adventure, shouldn't have recognized mystery in the oil and old exhaust fumes that lay just below her soft nostrils. But that must have been what happened, because at midafternoon she was two miles west of town, trotting steadily in front of a school bus full of admiring children, and by the supper hour, when the great silence fell, she was just outside the village.

The silence stopped everything. It was as if the bottom of the air had dropped underground, or as if the top of the jar that held the known world had lifted off.

In the parking area of Frenchie's Superette, two women in off-white sweaters stared at each other across the roofs of three cars, and the children on their hips stopped kicking. Maud Nash in her kitchen stopped stirring grape jelly into her plate of cottage cheese. Byron Doatze sat still in the high cab of his fuel-oil truck with his foot on the clutch and the key in his hand. The minister, Jim Parsons, lowered his bushel basket of apples to the sidewalk. All the cats in town woke up.

And then the cow began to run.

HER BONES aren't meant for it, the muscles that keep her joints from bursting apart aren't meant for it, her very eyes are set wrong on her head for such speed. She runs too hard, down the middle of the road into town. People see her now. Frenchie can see out the propped door of his Superette that will burn to the ground in the coming winter, and Mike Connor beside him sees too, who will be one of the volunteers holding a flaccid hose in the cold; then, in the little meadow the town calls Millet Green because once there was on it a shoe factory owned by Mr. Milette and Mr. Greene, over there that woman coming down the bank with her arms full of half-dry weeds, she sees; Old Will, drunk as he is, beside the post office, and across the road Lily the town cop's wife, and going down her driveway young Janet Rhodin who meant to step into the cemetery for a few minutes but got stopped by the silence, they see; up beyond and behind, across from Maude Nash's house, two children who were running away from the school playground toward supper when it stopped them too, and one of them still so hipless her pants hang jaunty and innocent about her; and just this side of them Jim Parsons leaning over his basket of apples that don't even smell because everything, even scent, has stopped moving in this whole universe except what they all see, that cow.

They haven't had time yet to think what the silence means, but she has come at her crazy plate-footed gallop into the silence as if it had occurred for her, and each of them lets her have it for as long as it takes her to pass. Even her running, so terrific and urgent, makes a sound round and wooden like silence, straight up the middle of the road. This flat-out running, stride after stride, is horses' business. The cow has no gait for it, and she has shut her eyes in despair. She can't stop running. Every bone is trying to get away from the pain of the crazed and stricken muscles, and the cow runs straight up the middle of the road with a tornado two miles behind her. Maude Nash, who came to Clayborne five years ago to be the librarian, has come to the window in her bathrobe to see the silence. She is standing at the window, she was fifty-three last July, she has walked the ramparts of her soul and found no grief she cannot bear, she sees the cow. Maude sees. Her bones are not made for it; the very eyes in her head are in the wrong place for seeing back or ahead. Her breath comes bitter. And Maude sees. Pity strikes Maude broadside, knocks the breath out of her in a single instant so her shout is sucked away into a sudden and desperate hoarseness, as the cow's broad feet slide and she stumbles back upright before she's all the way down. She bellows. Raises up her old head and still at the clumsy full-tilt run bellows out terrors, finds her feet on blessed grass again, veers up over the high school lawn that has become almost blue in the queer lighted dark that is dropping in.

She pulls the fear along behind her like a string of old tin cans tied to her tail, only half a mile ahead of the tornado now, and the people have seen her and they believe. They spring for the safety nearest. The child grabs her own belt loops as she runs, and Jim Parsons leaves his basket of apples twenty steps from his own front door. Frenchie says, "Holey moley!" "Yeah," says Mike. "Holey oley moley," says Frenchie.

IN THE HIGH cab of the oil truck, facing the empty pasture, Byron Doatze began to curse. "Goddamned heap!" he shouted at the windshield. He jammed down the gas pedal. "Asshole!" he shouted, and turned the key so hard it dug deep into the finger flesh between his calluses. He yanked the key out and threw it across the cab. "Shit box!" he shouted. The key bounced off the window onto the dashboard. The sloping dashboard. Byron lunged to catch the key. It dropped to the floor, and he heard it slide under the seat as the steering wheel grabbed his side and the stick shift rammed his chest. He sat back up and took the steering wheel in both big hands and shook it with his whole strength. "You goddamned hopeless godforsaken jerk!"

He was hale and hearty, barrel-chested, clean-shaven, square-headed and square-fisted and a square-dealing fuel-oil man. His hair was gray. He was stocky, he was sturdy, he was stalwart and tough. He had started driving home with a pair of pork chops and a hot shower on his mind, and then maybe a little trip to the Rainbow for a beer, maybe not. He threw open the door of his truck cab with such fury that the big truck rocked, and he jumped down, and slammed the door shut so hard that the truck stopped rocking. The noise of it was sharp in the silence that was almost over, but there was no echo at all.

Byron Doatze was a notable man: he was at that moment one of seven people who had heard the tornado warning on the radio, and his cow was gone, and his truck wasn't going to start until it had at least an hour's rest, and he was one of God's own patient men except for sometimes, like now, when he met more than he could bear and lost all his patience at once. He reached back with one steel-toed boot and kicked the truck. It almost knocked him down.

There had been another tornado years ago in Texas, a construction job he had after the army, two-by-fours sticking straight through the foreman's trailer office, like carnival swords through the box a lady was in, a dead poodle draped over a third-story girder. He had called home as soon as he could to tell them he was all right. They hadn't known there'd been a tornado at all, a couple thousand miles away, his father the coal man, the woman his father had married, and his younger brother Will. Two old ladies drowned in their own parlor, a little kid and a cat in a cellar with the house blown down upstairs.

Behind Byron's house, across the tops of the trees on the first hill, came a sudden darkening, as if a dye were being drawn slowly across. Byron looked, and he dreamed, for a long instant, his cow: lifted and turned on her side and sailing over thrashing maple trees, her tail straight out.

THE TORNADO came up to the far end of Clayborne and hopped, taking with it all the ashes from both working fireplaces in the old Wilcox place, where Jacob slept through the whole thing. It came down again just past the town line, turned Ike's Trash and Treasure Trailer upside down and inside out, carried off two chickens and possibly a pony harness from Mitchell's hired man's yard, and then got lost and petered out along the Tessamay River bed somewhere before Livingston. Behind it came a torrential rain and high winds that lasted a good hour.

Then the wind let up, but the rain kept on steady and hard for the rest of the night, and all the power was out. Byron Doatze spent two hours of the worst of it walking, hoping he was following his cow. Jim Parsons spent the worst of it standing in his living room holding a blue candle that he didn't have a match to light; then he gave up and went to bed. Maude Nash stood at her front-room window until some dark bird smashed into it, and then she came back to herself, found the flashlight and the candles, and she'd be damned if that storm was going to send her to bed hungry. She lit a can of Sterno in the chafing-dish base and put a kettle of water over it to boil while she finished her cottage cheese.

The cow had stopped running right after the funnel roared over and pulled in the rain behind it. She slowed to a skittery trot just past the tennis courts and then to a walk up the sideline of the football field, head down at last, tail down at last, only her hide still twitching in shimmers every time the lightning flashed. She walked on until she got into the protected bay of the bus garage, where she stood with the rain streaming and steaming off her until Byron appeared with a rope in his hands. Then she lowed, just once, a cautious complaint. Byron, whose patience had been restored by exertion and steady wet, told her what an almighty clever thing she was, thanked her for having left such a clear trail along the football field, and slipped the rope over her head.

Maude lifted the lid off the teakettle and shone the flashlight in. Bubbles were beginning to rise along the sides. She had figured on instant soup, maybe afterward some tea, and some cookies if she could find them. And if the candles turned out to give enough light, maybe she'd write a few letters. She closed the kettle back up. The sound of it clopping down went on.

That cow again.

She was on her way into the front room to take a look when Byron began to holler, "Hey! Hey! Here now! Hup!" just outside her front door. The cow took off at a spanking trot toward home, and Byron was all Maude saw, Byron left standing in the heavy rain with a rope in his hands.

"What the hell is he doing out there?" she said. He didn't move, just looked on down the road after his cow. Maude went and opened the front door.

"What the hell are you doing out there?" she called. He turned his head slowly, raised his hand to the visor of his cap, and was pushing it back when she yelled louder, thinking he hadn't heard over the rain, "Doatze! What the hell are you doing out there?"

"Ma'am?" he answered, and she realized he couldn't even see that her door was open, it was that dark everywhere except somehow in the middle of the road where he stood, getting rained on hard.

"It's Maude Nash! Now come in out of the rain," she called, and added more quietly but out loud, "you damned fool."

He still didn't move except to take his cap the rest of the way off.

"Thanks," he called back, "but I've got to get along." And he gestured with his cap off down the road, vaguely, as if he didn't quite believe he was answering a real person.

Maude pulled her bathrobe lapels together hard at her throat, stepped out into the rain on her top step, and yelled, "You darn fool, come here!"

His cap hesitated in midair, and then he put it back on and walked out of the road to the foot of Maude's front steps. Maude was known for doing such things, yelling like that. Children thought it was funny, a librarian who whispered in the library and yelled outdoors; some of them claimed they'd heard her talking to herself, but that was unlikely. She never talked to herself outside the unwilled privacy of her own neat little house, and rarely talked to herself inside it, though when she did, it didn't bother her.

She had stepped back inside the doorway as soon as she saw he was moving, and when he paused there at the foot of her steps in the pouring down rain, she got impatient. "Byron Doatze, for crying out loud get in here so I can shut this door and talk like a human!"

So he came up the steps and through the door and took off his cap again and dripped on the rug in her front hall. "I appreciate it," he said, "but I really got to go along and get ahold of that cow." He was hale and hearty, and not a soul in the whole town even wondered anymore why he had come back and stayed and never settled down with some woman or other. They didn't even wonder about the cow anymore, why old Doatze's son was bothering to feed and keep a cow that wouldn't breed, a barren old cow he couldn't even milk. The door behind him came closed, shutting off the noise of the rain outside, closing him, them, into the stillness of the house, and he stood there, the oil man in his raincoat, in the middle of the night it felt like, standing in odd Maude's house when he had work to do and the whole town was going to bed. Strong and sturdy and blushing like mad in the dark front hall.

Maybe this was something he'd been waiting for.

"That cow!" Maude said. "That was your cow, then. Which I prob-ably should have figured out. But you had a hold of her, didn't you?"

Because Maude was hale and hearty too, and she had seen the cow at her clattering gallop. And if Byron Doatze stood streaming now in her front hall, it was because she had too little work to do and too much vigor left after it was done. She'd have yelled into the rain for him to come in anyway, of course, since where she came from everybody yelled and nobody stood in the rain, but this whole damn town acted deaf to her. Maude was hospitable, but she was a square-dealing woman.

Byron nodded. "I did," he said. "I certainly did, for a minute or two. Then off she went, hell-bent for leather, heading for home once she saw where the road was." He patted his cap gently against his thigh.

"Well, if she's off for home, she's got sense enough to find it, and you better dry out or you'll have pneumonia."

She turned from his blush and walked, square-shouldered and square-hipped inside the old navy blue bathrobe, down the hall to the kitchen.

"Can you drink tea, or does it have to be coffee?" she asked. "And get out of that coat and boots before you come dripping all over my hardwood floors."

In this way she bullied him out of his blush and into her kitchen, and he took a chair at the table without being told.

"So, do you want some of this," she held up the soup envelope, "or did you eat?"

That pair of pork chops lay in his refrigerator, next to a bowl of boiled potatoes. Assuming that the cow was going straight on home, he was no more than an hour away from his own supper. He cleared his throat.

"No, thank you, ma'am, I had a bite."

She lowered the packet.

"Before," he added.

"Byron Doatze, so help me, don't you call me ma'am one more time," she said. Her voice was calm, friendly, as if she were inviting him to draw the best easy chair close to the fire and make himself at home, with just a little warning that the right front leg wobbled so he should lift it when he pulled. "I've got names enough for you to choose one, and you know what they are, and I don't care what you call me so long as it isn't ma'am. And if you don't want soup you can go hungry." He stared at the top of her head as she aimed the flashlight into the teakettle again and peered at the steam. "And I don't mean to go on calling you Byron Doatze like a Quaker all night, either. What do they call you?" She shut the flashlight off and settled the lid back before she even looked at him.

Byron looked her full in the face for a long time it seemed, across the teakettle and the blue flame and the light of the five candles. "They call me Mr. Doatze," he said evenly.

Without even cracking a smile, he stood up, slowly, pushed his chair back a little, crossed his arms over his lower chest, bent slightly forward, and said in falsetto, for all the world just like Frenchie's skinny wife in her eternal cardigan sweater, "Mr. Doatze! Mr. Doughatss! My husband said you take care you don't knock that forsythia again!"

Then he sat down, a man not known for his wit, and scooted his chair back up to the table while Maude Nash laughed, no more worried than she ever was about how loud she did it or how many of her teeth showed.

When she'd stopped laughing he said, "Byron," and she said, "Maude," and they shook hands across her kitchen table.

She got him to say he'd drink some instant coffee, and he told her how he hadn't even bothered to tighten up the rope around the cow's neck.

He chuckled. "She was so blamed glad to see me, dripping cold up there by the bus barns, I never thought she'd figure on taking off like that, but *whoo!* first second she feels that road under her feet it's like she knows the way home after all, and away she goes. Surprised me more than a little, that's for sure."

"She surprised the whole town when she came through ahead of that storm. Surprised me, at least. It's a wonder she didn't kill herself, galloping along like a racehorse." Maude shook her head.

"She's a good cow for all that. Quiet around the house."

If they'd known each other an hour or so better, Maude might have tapped him on the shoulder.

"Not so quiet tonight, though."

"Well," he said, "can't expect her to be still in the middle of a tornado."

"So that's what it was? Officially?"

He nodded. By then he was getting comfortable and hungry, and as they talked he helped himself to the saltines she had on the table for her soup. She got up and went to the cupboard to get him a cup for his coffee. "You think you've got room for cookies?" she asked over her shoulder. "Or did you have too big a supper Before?"

"What kind of cookies?" he said.

"Lost cookies—I've put them somewhere, and I may be able to find them, or I may not."

"Yes, please," he said, and they both laughed, and then he said, "Have you ever tried a cookie jar?"

Maude put the cup of coffee in front of him and sat down. "Boring," she said. "Predictable."

"Convenient," he said.

"But you're not hungry, as we've established."

Byron sipped his coffee and nodded. "Though, I admit, it's a long time since I had lost cookies. A long time." He squinted at the candle flames. "A man could work up an appetite for a rare delicacy like that."

"Macaroni," she said, pointing at him and grinning, and she got up and pulled open a drawer, and found the package of chocolate cookies under a bag of egg noodles.

"Sure," he said.

"Spoil your supper, see if I care." She poured the cookies into a bowl and set them on the table. She looked at them for a second and then said, "Napkins, I suppose."

"Napkins?"

"Well, you're company, aren't you?"

He leaned back a little. "I suppose I am. Uninvited, though—maybe there's got to be an invitation for it to mean napkins."

She scowled, playing. " 'Get in here' counts, I think, as an invitation. So," she took a candle and went out of the kitchen for a minute and came back with two white cloth napkins. "There," she said, and put one down beside his hands.

"No fine china?" he said.

"No shoes, no fine china," she said. "Now, tell me the story of your life."

He unfolded the napkin and spread it on his lap. "Born in Clayborne, grew up here, went away, came back. You?"

"Born in Brooklyn, grew up there, came here. That was illuminating."

"You play cards?"

"No."

"Neither do I. Your turn."

She snorted.

"You know," he said, "I don't think I was ever inside this house before. It's nice."

"Thank you—I like it. Good light. In the daytime."

"Talbots used to live here when I was a kid. He was the postmaster—I remember them as old, but maybe they weren't. I remember we soaped the windows one Halloween—I remember that for certain."

"That was neighborly of you."

"Well, nobody liked him, and his wife was kind of mean. At least, being kids, we thought she was. She used to holler at kids who walked on her grass."

"Well, it wasn't their grass," Maude said.

"Actually, I don't even know if she really did holler. I never heard her do it. But people said so." He grinned. "And that one Halloween they were out of town. We did a good job. My brother Will did the low parts, and I did the high parts. Every one of those," and he pointed back into the living room. "And besides," he said, "they weren't neighbors—they lived in town and we lived outside of town. Two entirely different worlds. Bussers and walkers."

Maude shrugged, took another cookie. "Where does Will live now?"

Byron felt his pant legs to see how they were drying out. "Oh, he lives here in town. We don't see each other." Though he was seeing Will, even as he said it: Old Will, people called him, already, Old Will, standing in front of the beer cooler in Frenchie's Superette, counting the coins in his hand, swaying, reeking. Sweet William, their mother had called him.

And Maude was suddenly aware of the sound of her own chewing, an awareness that irritated her, so she chewed harder, taking her time, and then she swallowed, and touched her napkin to the corners of her mouth before she said, "Families are a mixed blessing."

"Where's yours?" Byron said.

She flapped her hand in the air. "Everywhere," she said. "Except here."

"Miss them?"

"Some of them—we were five girls and a boy. I'm the oldest. I like two of my sisters."

He laughed. "Not such a great percentage," he said.

"I wouldn't talk," she said, but she was smiling. "I don't know—their lives went differently. They all got married, had kids. We send cards on holidays."

"Your parents?"

"Both gone, a long time now. And don't say you're sorry."

"Okay."

But something had already happened, and they both knew it: by accident they had moved from some first level of easy joking friendship to some second level, and for a few moments they sat quietly, sipped from their cups. By accident, certainly, but not, each of them felt, without some intention.

"So," she said, "that was a tornado."

"It was."

"My first," she said.

"My second," he said.

"Really."

"Years ago when I was in Texas I was in another one that was a lot worse."

She could hear something offering in his voice, and something surprisingly impatient in her own: "What were you doing in Texas?"

"Construction work. After the army."

"All right," she said, and put her hand flat on the table. "So you were born here, went into the army, went to Texas."

He nodded, almost grinning. He had a suspicion of what she wanted to know, and a suspicion that he wanted to know the same thing. "Came back."

She drummed her fingers. "Came back, built a peculiar little house out of fieldstones, live with a cow."

"Right," he said. "Live with a cow." Then he took another cookie and a deep breath. "And you never got married either."

"I never did," she said. "Never missed it, that I know of," she said, and both of them could hear an odd softness in her voice. "I'm a good aunt," she offered, and they both laughed. "Seriously—" She patted her lapels. "I like a life where I can come home and change into my bathrobe and do whatever I want to until I fall asleep."

He nodded. "Living alone, you get that kind of habit. I suppose you get other kinds if you don't live alone. Maybe they're just as good, but—well, I've got my cow," he said, and they both smiled. "She was lucky about that tornado," he said. He put his hand up, flat, beside one of the candle flames, feeling the spot of heat, and then put his hand back in his lap. "My mother—well, we kept cows when I was a kid. And she was fond of them."

Maude wanted to say something about what her mother had been fond of, but she couldn't find it. "I never even imagined having children," she said, "but I always wanted to be an aunt—I wanted to be the one who'd send a child the perfect, unexpected, life-changing gift."

"Did you have an aunt like that?"

"Nope—but I read about them," she said.

"Well, then. That explains the library," he said.

All this time the rain kept on out in the night, and they felt how the time was going on. And then, in the light of five candles and a can of Sterno in the kitchen of the dark house, Byron said, "There's a basket of apples sitting beside the road in front of the church."

"Is there?"

He nodded. "There is. Now, I imagine they belong to Mister Parsons."

"Parson Parsons," she said.

"Parson Parsons," he agreed.

"Does he know it's funny?"

He pushed cookie crumbs together on the table with his fingers and shook his head. "Nope," he said.

"Oh, come on," she said. "He has to know it's funny."

"Known him all my life. Man doesn't know anything funny."

"How about Dan Ward, then? Ward the Warden?"

Byron grinned again, rubbed the side of his face. "Well, I have to admit I hadn't noticed that one. Probably because I think of him as the guy who wants a drainage ditch, instead of thinking he's a cop."

"Now," she said, "I know I'm a foreigner, I know I have peculiar ideas—but can you tell me why in the name of all that's holy a town this poor is paying a salary to a policeman?"

Byron shook his head, smiling, not really thinking about Dan, thinking instead about how to ask where she got the small scar that split her left eyebrow: he thought he liked it, though it made her look like she was about to laugh at a joke nobody else understood. "Constable," he said.

"Oh, for heaven's sake, constable, then," she said, though she too was thinking less about Dan than about how Byron had held his palm beside the flame, how the gesture had been both an inquiry and a caress. "The thing is," she said, "there's no traffic light, no stop sign—no traffic, for crying out loud, except when there's a parade, and then he's in the parade, not directing traffic."

He nodded. He liked her, her laugh and her kitchen, and the plain bossy way she had. "What about crime?" he said.

"Crime!" she said. "There's no crime, no traffic, therefore no need for a constable with a car. Name me a crime in Clayborne's history."

He rubbed his forehead, pinched the bridge of his nose carefully. "Escaped cow," he said. She laughed, but he nodded, keeping his face serious. "Need could arise," he said, "any minute."

And then the clock in Maude's living room chirred and rang its chimes: midnight.

They'd known all along that this moment had to come, of course, with all those circumstances being satisfied, right down to the candlelight. Byron Doatze was the oil man, but he'd been through two tornadoes now and lived in a narrow stone house he'd built for himself alone, and he knew he was with a woman in her nightclothes in the middle of the night. Maude Nash was the librarian, but she had a freshet beside her house every spring where the water ran so fast and cold that just to hear it raised and quenched thirst at once, and she knew she'd made him come in out of the rain, and she liked him, his voice and his hands, and she admired that he knew enough to keep that cow of his.

So they'd been hurrying a little the last while, feeling the moment coming on when there'd have to be a move one way or the other. They were stalwart, Maude and Byron. They were square-dealing people, too old to make believe they hadn't thought about what might happen, and about what it might mean, and about the moments of loneliness they could remember.

So they both had their hands on the table and nothing to say, and they both took a look. They sat there. Maude took her look, and Byron took his look. They both saw, because they could still see so clearly in spite of the candles and the rain and the dark and the nightclothes and Byron's sock feet, that it would be pretty hard to get from where they were into bed together. They saw that this, after all, was coffee and cookies and a warm dry house in a rainstorm, in spite of the tornado and the cow.

So Maude said, "I've got an umbrella I can loan you," and Byron said, "No, that's all right. I've got the raincoat. And besides, I'd probably lose it before I got it back to you."

BESIDE THE oil truck, the cow is asleep on her feet. A mile away, Byron is walking home, steady as the rain. In the neat yellow house back in the village, Maude is clearing the dishes to the sink. She wads up the cookie package and drops it into the wastebasket. "You damn fool," she says, almost smiling, just sad enough that she's not sure who she means. She blows out three candles and takes the other two with her upstairs.

Byron walks down his long driveway and smiles to see his cow. "You damn jerk," he says, and wakes her and leads her back behind her fence before he goes on to the house. He takes off his wet things in the dark, and walks through his kitchen into his tiny bedroom, where the rain falls past the deep window, and when he looks out into the dark he's not quite sure if it's his cow he's checking on.

And then the cow sighs, and goes back to sleep.

The Dummy

"BUSY NIGHT," Byron said, over the noise, when Brenda set his beer on the bar in front of him.

"For a weeknight," she agreed. "Hear you found that little deaf boy."

"Yup," he said, and raised the bottle in a mock toast.

Brenda gave the bar a pat. "On the house—excuse me," she said, and went to wait on somebody else. He watched her go, sorry, vaguely and not for the first time, that he wasn't the least bit in love with her. She reminded him pleasantly of a girl in Texas, almost fifteen years before.

"Hey, Doatze," Mike Connor called from down the bar.

Byron nodded back at him, and then at the other men with him, who raised hands or beers in greeting.

Most weeknights when Byron came in, he could stand at the bar and joke with Brenda for three beers and be interrupted only once or twice—the place stayed that quiet. But tonight, as if the tornado two days ago, or last night's search, had changed even the Rainbow, the place was so full he could hardly hear himself think.

Brenda went behind the bar again, uncapped a fresh beer, and set it in front of him. "It's on Frenchie," she said, pointing toward the back of the barroom.

"I'll be damned," Byron said, because Frenchie'd never bought anybody a beer, and that made Brenda laugh, so he said, "I better get out of here before chickens grow teeth."

"Oh, you," Brenda said, taking a little slap at his shoulder.

Then somebody called her. Byron caught Frenchie's eye, raised the second beer, and nodded his thanks.

Maybe it was that—thanking somebody he didn't like for something he didn't want—or maybe it was the noise in a place he preferred quiet, but he'd come for something else, and he didn't know what. He took another swallow and gave up. Next thing he knew he'd be feeling sorry for himself, and even as he thought that, he thought of Maude Nash and how she'd made fun of him the night before last in her kitchen. What a clean, surprising thing talking with her had been. And she didn't remind him at all of that old lost chance in Texas.

He pulled a dollar from his pocket and tucked it under his bottle. He hadn't planned on giving Brenda a blow-by-blow of the search, but there were a few things he'd have liked the chance to say, maybe just to hear how they sounded. And he sure didn't want to say them to Frenchie, or Mike, or any of the rest of them.

" 'Night," he called to Brenda, and she looked up, surprised for a second. Then she waved, and he waved and left.

He had spent the day tuning his truck's engine, so when he turned the key, it started right up, and now he tried to take some satisfaction in that, sitting there, listening to how smooth it was. But even as he listened, he grew aware that he was paying attention to listening, not to the engine, so he pulled the truck around and headed back toward town. His own house, which he had built himself, of stone, and where he lived alone, was a mile in the other direction, but he wasn't ready for that much quiet just yet, and he wasn't sure what he did want.

For a long minute at the four-way stop he considered turning down East Main and seeing if Maude was home. It was still early, maybe eight o'clock. The night of the tornado, night before last, she'd called him into her house to take shelter from the rain, bullied and bossed him into her kitchen, and sat there talking with him about nothing for hours. He'd known who she was for years, but this was the first time he'd talked to her, and when he left, she'd offered to lend him her umbrella. If he'd taken it—well, then he could have returned it, and she'd ask about the boy, and he could say this and that. And then? He remembered her strong, laughing face there in the candlelight in the middle of the night: the electricity out, she in her bathrobe and he in his socks. They'd talked and had a good time. No foolishness about Maude Nash, candlelight or not. He smiled. "Smart woman," he said aloud. She had a funny way of tilting her head when she was listening, and the candlelight had shown the white in her dark hair, had softened the small scar that split one eyebrow and made her look critical in the daylight.

All those requirements for romance had been satisfied, and what he'd felt, what they'd both felt, was simply comfortable. So he hadn't taken the umbrella, and he knew why, and she knew why. So he didn't have it to return, and that was that.

He turned east anyway, and saw that the lights were out in her house, and then he turned his truck around at the high school and drove past Nobel Aldrich's house, where Aldrich's car was in the driveway and the lights were on, upstairs and down. Man's got sense, Byron thought.

The night before, he and Nobel had been one of the search teams assigned to Clayborne Woods, the team that took the old logging road in, the team that found the boy and walked him out of the woods. Nobel had seen what Byron saw, and had had the sense to stay home tonight.

Meaning I don't, he thought then. Celebrating, for crying out loud (he was thinking now of all the men at the Rainbow). And why not: a five-year-old child had been lost; the men of the town had gotten together a search; they'd found the kid and he was fine. Why not celebrate?

29

Because. If Kyle had been a normal little kid and they'd found him crying, if he or Nobel had picked him up and said, "Hey there, little fellow, it's okay. Let's go find your momma, okay?" and held a bandanna so he could blow his nose, all right: go ahead and celebrate. The other fellows probably didn't see the difference, and no reason why they should. But he and Nobel Aldrich had been there, and that's why he wasn't celebrating, and why he felt a little ashamed that he'd gone to the Rainbow in the first place, and admired Nobel Aldrich for staying home.

IT WAS A mild night for September, moonlit, as the previous night had been, the night of the search. When he got home, his barren Holstein cow stood near the board fence, one hind leg delicately bent. He walked across the yard and reached over the fence to scratch the white center of her broad, hard forehead, taking in the good, deep, familiar smell of hay, manure, and cow. "Might as well tell you," he said, grinning to think what Maude would say about that, but then something like the upward swoop of being in love scooped into his stomach and throat, and for a second he thought he was going to cry.

He stroked the cow's black ear, running it through his fisted hand, feeling how warm and thick and tough it was, the coarse hairs distinct against his palm, and she didn't shake him off. The moonlight lay on the roof of the shed. "I guess all I was ready for was not to find him," he said. "I probably expected we'd hear the signal that somebody else had. Or that nobody would, and the search would get to be one of those long, ugly ones, and next spring his body would show up. But I didn't expect to find him sitting there like that with that dummy." He rubbed his thumb against the grain of the soft inside hairs of the cow's ear, smoothed them, and then let the ear slide free. He leaned his forearms on the fence and clasped his hands loosely together.

"So it made me feel strange. Right then, and it just keeps on. I've been trying to figure out what he was thinking. I don't know anything else to do about it. Probably the smart thing to do is talk to Nobel, see what his read on it was, a man with kids of his own and all."

He shrugged, looking past the cow's bony back. "Seems stupid, though. Don't know why, but it does." He sighed, opened his hands, and looked at his palms. "You take this boy, deaf and dumb since he was born, and here he is, four miles from home in the woods, lost, it's getting dark, and he's sitting there with a dummy. What does he think it is? Ventriloquists. They pretend they're not talking, make you believe the dummy's talking. He can't talk, can't hear. What does he think—it's just a doll or something?"

He stood up straight and looked the cow in the eye. "And he wasn't playing, either. That's the thing."

The cow switched her tail slowly and shifted her weight.

"He wasn't playing. I never saw anybody more serious than that boy was."

Byron rubbed his hand over his jaw while the moon hung steady and the cow stood still.

"Here's how I figure it," he said. "Here's what I think happened."

And then he was silent for a long minute, seeing in his mind how the boy and his mother would have been just sitting around in Ike's yard, a nice day, sunshine, the boy probably with a toy truck, Louise having a glass of tea and chatting, Ike opening a box somebody had just dropped off.

"The boy, Kyle, he's watching, curious, even though it's the kind of stuff Ike does all the time—unpacking the junk people bring him, the leftovers of their yard sales, whatever.

"Sure he's curious. You've got to think what the Trash and Treasure Trailer looks like to a kid. This fat old trailer just full of all that kind of junk Ike had. Old hats, a birdcage, trunks full of busted toys, rusted tools."

Byron smiled and leaned on the fence again, easy. "You know, one time when he was little, Will told me that when he grew up, Dad would grow down." He smiled again, thinking of Will big and Dad little, of Will, his brother, when they'd still been boys together. "Well," he said softly. "Well, so kids figure things out the way it makes sense to them. And maybe it seemed to Kyle that when he grew up, he would get the trailer, get to keep all that stuff. Or maybe he had some money from birthdays or something, and he figured he could buy some of Ike's stuff."

He sighed. "If he knows about buying. That's the thing—you can't tell what he knows, how he figures things out."

Byron thought again of Kyle in the dark woods—when they turned the flashlights on him and he froze, and then stood up, not scrambling up like a scared kid but getting to his feet, almost like a man would.

The cow sighed, her stomachs sounding.

"Anyway. So Ike opens the box. It's got some other junk in it— maybe old Christmas decorations, curtains—but then Ike lifts out this dummy." Byron could see the dummy's face as he had seen it in the woods, menacing and tragic, could smell the old wet leaves. He tried hard to imagine it in sunlight, as Kyle would have seen it, with his mother nearby, nothing scary about it, and not knowing what it was for.

"It's a boy, wearing a brown tweed jacket and brown trousers, and it's almost as big as Kyle. Ike holds it up, and its arms and legs dangle down, and he gives it a little shake. He says, 'Look at this,' and Louise looks and she says she hates it—'I hate those things,' she says. 'They're weird.'

"Ike says it's a collector's item. That's how Ike is. He'd say that. He'd say, 'It looks a little like that what's-his-name—Charlie McCarthy.' And Louise wouldn't buy that. Charlie McCarthy wore a top hat. This one's ugly, and it's got a smart-aleck face, and its hair's all ratty. But Ike puts his hand into the hole in the dummy's back and makes it blink.

"And the kid doesn't know what they're saying, but he's watching now. Ike makes the mouth open and shut, like he's the ventriloquist, and he screws his face all up and says, 'Hey there, kid—what you lookin' at?'

"Louise says 'Don't,' but it's too late—Ike makes the dummy wink at Kyle. It's too late. Ike makes the dummy look back at Louise, makes it say, 'Whatza matter, lady—you don't like dummies?' and Louise says, 'Don't use that word,' and Ike goes red, because he didn't mean anything, and he says, 'No offense,' and he takes his hand out and puts the thing down on the grass. And it lies there for the rest of the afternoon, while they unpack the other boxes and have another glass of tea.

"Maybe they notice how the boy lies there near it; maybe they don't. Maybe they should have known right off when he disappeared that he'd gone after it, but they're not really paying attention, maybe. It's got to be easy to ignore a kid who doesn't talk to you and can't hear when you talk to him."

The cow shook her head, began to chew, and stepped closer to the fence.

"I don't know—Louise loves him, no doubt there, and she's a good mother. Maybe she did notice, and then the tornado just shook everything up so it slipped her mind. So when he came up missing, she thought he'd been stolen.

"In a way, I guess, he had been. Lying there on the hot grass, watching that dummy lying there on the hot grass."

Byron stroked the cow's dusty neck absently, seeing in his mind the oddly rough skin of the dummy's face, the heavily painted eyebrows, the full smirking lips, how the flashlight had picked up the shine of the paint and made the eyes glitter.

"He knew the dummy wasn't alive. I'm sure about that. But there's something about those things. He'd probably be careful not to stare too hard, for fear it would turn and look at him again. Maybe he felt kind of sorry for it." He rubbed his palm over the bony top of the cow's head. "Maybe one time his mother took her fingers and lifted the corners of his mouth to make him smile, and he kept his face like that, like the dummy's was now, all the time they were in some place where he knew his mother wanted him to smile, and he remembered how sad he'd been. So maybe he lay there on the grass and thought how he'd like to push the dummy's grin down, so the face could relax."

The cow lowered her head and stepped away from his hand. The moon had moved, and Byron was thinking about the time Mom had done that, had not said a word, just forced his mouth into a smirk, and he'd kept it that way, all through the long afternoon of his sister Kate's getting married. Damned if he knew why she had, to this day.

"That's probably just me, you're right," he said to the cow's profile. "What the hell do I know what he thought? I don't even know what I think half the time. And here I am, talking to a cow—not much better off than him, am I?"

Byron dusted his palms against each other and put his hands in his pockets. "Talking to your cow, By," he said, and tried to laugh, to dodge the return of that sad, sweet feeling.

"What you need . . . ," he said, and didn't bother to finish. He got into his truck again and headed back to the Rainbow. It would have to be emptied out by now, probably almost nine o'clock. Better than nothing, he thought; and then, because he was a decent and honest man, he thought, No offense, for Brenda had always been as nice to him as she could be.

AS HE DROVE, he thought, That's me too, not the kid. But he couldn't stop imagining Kyle lying in bed in the dark, being little, thinking of how next time they went across the road to the trailer, he would find the dummy and refuse to be parted from it. He'd hug it, hug that scratchy brown jacket, and the body would be against his, just sticks inside the clothes. That would give him a strange feeling in his stomach, but he would hold on. And when his mother carried him home, her throat moving with talk, he would bring the dummy with him.

The boy imagining theft: While Ike was asleep, he could look both ways and go across the road and go into the trailer and find the dummy, take its odd body in his arms, and carry it home. It wouldn't be too heavy. And then he would have it in his room.

And thinking of frightening his mother: He had seen Ike put his hand into the dummy's back, and if he had the dummy in his room, he could figure out how it worked. When he had figured it out, he would go into the room where his mother was sleeping and shake her by the shoulder, and when she opened her eyes, he would put the face of the dummy in front of her face and chop its toothy mouth open and shut and scare her. Then he felt very bad and frightened himself, because he knew how warm she smelled in the morning in her bed, and he imagined that when she got scared, she might cry: she had cried once, and he had cried too. Now, alone in the bed, he shook his head. No, if he had that thing, he wouldn't scare her with it. She didn't like it, he knew that much. And she did like him.

But none of that's anything but me, Byron thought, and he didn't even put on his turn signal, because there were so many cars and pickups still in the Rainbow's parking lot. He drove on into town, listening to his truck's motor and trying not to think of Kyle thinking about the dummy's head, the face. How that rough, shiny skin would feel to his tongue if he got a chance to lick it. How cool and hard the grinning cheek would be against his own. Byron said aloud, "Knock it off," and wished that he had a radio in the truck. He drove past the feed store, past Poole's Ford dealership with the plastic pennants, past the Mobil station and the dark doughnut shop, and on into the center of town, where Maude Nash was just locking the library and coming down the steps. He pulled over on the wrong side of the street and called softly to her, "Ride?"

And there she was, Maude, not startled or even answering, just coming around to the other side of the truck in an ordinary way, the truck's headlights making the white flowers on her full skirt glow for a second as she passed. He leaned over and pushed the door open for her, thinking how strange it was that he wasn't worried about whether she'd have trouble with the high step into the cab—that he wasn't worried about a thing. She slid her books onto the seat and climbed up and in, slamming the door with a strong pull. She had on lipstick and her hair was wavier, combed back more carefully, but her eyes were no different. They still looked right at him, and in the dim cab light the funny eyebrow asked only the gentlest, most patient question.

"Nice night for walking," she said, observed, greeted.

And so, even though he could smell faint perfume and a slight nostalgic scent of the library, paste and paper and wood, he could say, as if they'd been having easy conversations for years, "Like to show you something, if you've got time. Out past—well, out past where Ike's Trash and Treasure used to be."

She nodded, an ordinary nod, simple, turning her face to look out the windshield, as if they were already on their way. "Where you found little Kyle," she said.

"Yes," he said. He put the truck in gear and drove.

After they'd passed her house and the high school and the old depot, she said, "I'd wondered about that," but not in a way that needed an answer, so he drove on. The two miles from the edge of the village to the lights in Ike's house were quiet except for the truck's smooth engine and the tires on the asphalt. The moonlight showed up once the houses thinned out.

"Looks funny without the trailer," she said—and it did, Ike's little house oddly naked to the road. The space in front of it, where the trailer had sat for twenty-some years until the tornado came and turned it inside out and upside down, looked too small for anything to have been there. Now only some chunks of twisted metal and some broken glass were left. Even the cinder blocks it had sat on were gone.

"It does," Byron said. "Pretty lucky it missed both houses." He slowed and put on his signal a quarter mile past Ike's. "Little bumpy here," he said, apologetically, and eased the truck off the shoulder and into Newton's cornfield. The headlights showed the neat rows of cornstalk stubble angling off from the wagon track.

Maude said, "I imagine the search would have been harder if it had happened before the corn was cut," and Byron, who hadn't thought of that, could see what she meant: acres and acres of corn whispering, taller than the men, dense, impossible to search. Just thinking of it, he felt again the small panic of the night before, when he and Nobel had started back with the boy between them and he had for an instant believed that they were headed wrong, that the trees should have thinned by now.

A lot of luck in this whole thing, he thought of saying, the sentence in his head, but he didn't. He shifted down into second, his headlights showing the trees a quarter mile ahead, and said nothing. He brought the truck to a stop ten feet from the first trees, shifted into neutral, put on the hand brake, and turned on his high beams.

THE TREES HERE were mostly young maples and skinny walnuts and wild crab apples. Behind them were older maples and a few dogwoods and oaks and hemlocks—an ordinary woods, with a path in and some honeysuckle and probably poison ivy in the undergrowth. But things hung from the trees, things that had never hung from trees before.

A bent black umbrella, its handle carved like a duck's head. A limp embroidered felt sombrero, rinsed pink, and a huge green lampshade, one side caved in. A blue tablecloth draped like bunting from one tree to another, gold threads in it sparkling in the headlights. A white plastic doll stroller, a dish drainer, a flowered bathrobe hung as neatly from a spruce branch as if it had been on a bathroom door, a throw pillow with its stuffing dangling like a cloud, a work boot, part of a fishing rod.

And on the path itself a gray portable typewriter, driven half into the ground; the top of a pressure cooker, its round gauge like a monocle; silverware; a glass doorknob; the round wire cage from a Bingo set.

All this in the moonlight, in the headlights.

"Good God," Maude said.

It had been sundown by the time he and Nobel had reached here, and dusky among the trees. A trace of fog had risen along the ground, and they had both paused right there at the edge of the trees, touching their flashlights before they went in. First thing, he had stepped on a sodden stuffed animal and started back, feeling its softened shape as flesh under his foot. And then, seeing what it really was, a light blue bear or dog with a limp ribbon around its neck, he'd gone on two or three steps before stumbling against the typewriter. Nobel had said, "Have to watch our step in here," and turned on his flashlight, even though it was plenty light enough to see, if they paid attention. They'd gone in along the trail maybe half a mile before the things the tornado had flung out of the Treasure Trailer began to thin out, began to be only a rag here and there, a baseball cap, a torn paper fan.

"He followed the things," Byron said. "Like they were a trail he was on. Clues." That wasn't at all what he had meant to say, and for the first time since he had pulled over by the library, he was uneasy. What was he doing, anyway? Farther down the path, he knew, lay marbles and the broken wooden cigar box they must have been in, a swollen book of piano music, a plaid sneaker. Off to the right, somewhere in the undergrowth, where he had kicked it in a reflex of fear, was a snakelike bicycle tire.

But Maude said, "Like Hansel and Gretel," quietly, the shock gone out of her voice, and Byron said, "Yes—like that. Hunting that dummy."

"Dummy."

As they watched, the truck's motor humming, a broken gilt picture frame slid from a high place in a hemlock and hit the ground, separating into slats.

"We didn't know about it when we were looking. It was an old ventriloquist's dummy from the Trash and Treasure, blown out with everything else. He was looking for it. Nobel Aldrich and I went in along this trail about two miles, slow and quiet, listening for him, looking with our flashlights. Then we decided to come back—to spread out to either side of the trail about ten or twelve yards and come back that way."

That far in, the ground fog had been gone, and Byron had kept feeling that wet dog or whatever it was he'd stepped on, the weird weakening of his leg muscles as his foot hit it, had kept waiting for the real snake that the bicycle tire hadn't been. It had been so quiet that he wondered now if he'd been thinking anything at all. He'd listened to the noise he made and the noise Nobel made, invisible twenty-five yards away except for the flashlight now and then.

"We were walking along as quiet as we could in there, trying to listen for him if he was crying or walking—not much else we could do," Byron said. He couldn't even begin to explain the kind of quiet it had been, as if the silence were a transparent absence, a clear waiting shape made by the crossings of branches and stems. Or what had happened in his throat and stomach when he heard the sound, how hard it had been to force his brain and then his mouth, tongue, throat, to call, "Nobel?" Nobel had stopped, and the silence had been sharp edged, like held breath, even after Nobel called back, "Yeah?" and Byron called, "I think we got something."

"I heard this sound—this quiet little *tup tup tup* sound. Sort of wooden sounding, not like a bird or an insect but steady, and then it would stop for a few seconds and start up again." The headlights made the yellow glass eye in the umbrella handle gleam. "I looked over to the right and I saw something move and then I saw him sitting there by a big old maple with this ventriloquist's dummy."

The boy had seemed to glow softly, his bare arms and legs, his blond head. All that paleness there in the dusk beside that dark old tree. He was sitting cross-legged, half toward the path, holding the dummy facing him, so that Byron had seen the dummy's face before he saw the boy's. The dummy's eyes had glittered as its thick lips opened and no sound came out. Nobel had come up beside Byron then, his flashlight, like Byron's, pointing down, as if they both knew that they had found something not to shine a light on.

"It was the strangest thing I ever saw. He had his hand in the back of the dummy, and what I'd heard was the dummy's mouth clopping shut—open, shut, open, shut." Byron moved his hand, flat fingered, to show how the mouth had gone, but it was wrong—it was the silhouette of a quacking duck, silly. He put his hand back on the steering wheel. "The boy was making the dummy move its mouth for a while—like for a sentence, maybe—and then he moved his mouth the same way." Something small and dark, mouse or mole, rolled like a dustball across the path. "Up and down, up and down." How empty the boy had made his face to get his jaw to move that way.

Maude drew in a breath and let it out without saying anything, and Byron couldn't tell whether he was glad or not that she hadn't spoken. But he knew that the ease he'd felt with her the other night, sitting in her kitchen and deciding he'd had too good a time to spoil it by making suggestions, and watching her deciding the same thing—that ease was gone. To keep the sad lonesomeness of knowing that from filling him up, he started talking again, saying random things, looking at the junk hanging in the trees and sparkling on the path.

"I never knew Louise to speak of. Knew her dad some years ago, but I didn't know she was back in town. Ike said they'd been out looking for an hour, and she just kept calling and calling, like the boy could hear her. Ike was out of patience, I think, but I bet if he'd been looking alone he'd have been calling too. You feel stupid not calling—have to make yourself not do it."

He could feel Maude looking at him now, watching his face by the dim dashboard light, but he kept his eyes on the round gleam of the pressure-cooker gauge and his hands on the wheel. "First thing, there's this tornado, and no way Louise could explain it to him, make him understand why all of a sudden they're sitting down in the basement and it's dark at suppertime. Supper's on the table, and they're sitting on the basement floor. He can't hear the wind. I don't know, maybe she's got some way of talking to him. He's five, got to have figured something out by now—maybe he knows about storms from the vibrations. Maybe when the tornado went over and picked that trailer up and threw it, he knew exactly what was going on. Maybe he knows people talk and hear and he doesn't, but I keep thinking about it, and I can't make it make sense. It's like one of us suspected that other people could do something with their knees that meant something, or their elbows, that we couldn't do and couldn't even imagine—"

Maude laughed then—not her big roaring laugh, that he'd heard at her kitchen table when they'd been joking about Frenchie's skinny wife, but a gentle little laugh.

"Sorry," she said, but she was smiling. "It just sounded funny. Talking with our elbows." She looked back out, and now Byron watched her, seeing the delicate skin beside her eyes, the deep waves of her hair, the way her eyebrows moved when she talked. "You know, the first ventriloquists were fortune-tellers," she said. "Prophets. Probably Moses was a ventriloquist—the burning bush and all that." She glanced at him and then away, and in Byron's chest the loop of sadness turned and sprang, arched near his throat.

TWO NIGHTS AGO, in her kitchen, a moment had come, a little past midnight, when they'd looked at each other, clear and simple, and seen that they weren't in love. They hadn't said it, but that's what it was, and so she'd offered her umbrella, and he'd said thank you, no. And now this was another moment. Byron drew a long breath, looked out at the spangled blue cloth in the trees, and said the one thing he hadn't thought.

"I think he was in love with it," he said.

Out of the corner of his eye he saw her hand lift itself from her lap in a little flutter, not even close to high enough to touch her throat. But that's the gesture it was, stopped, held down.

But all she said was "So. When you found him . . . ," which brought back the boy and the heavy-lidded eyes of the dummy, the pale yellow of the flashlight beam. And Byron said, "It was just so private. But he—" Then he had to stop, had to put both his hands over his eyes and smooth his face, down and out, feeling the roughness of his fingertips on his eyelids, his palms on his cheeks, the day's stubble against his palms.

He and Nobel had both kept their lights down and had moved to the right, so that they could see the boy's face before they approached. Five years old. The sweetest mouth, that fragile neck, and the way he looked into that dummy's eyes. The way he was waiting.

"I don't know how to describe it," he said. "For just a couple of seconds I got to see him working at it—looking into that dummy's eyes and moving his mouth. Not like he was saying words. Just open and shut, just like the dummy's mouth did. Open and shut. And then he saw my light and he stopped. But he kept on looking into those eyes for a second. And I don't have any idea what he was thinking." He ran his palms along the steering wheel. "None of my business."

He turned his hands over and looked at his palms, the darkness of the palms, the calluses. "I guess some things you can't explain," he said.

Byron waited a long time, it seemed, in the humming quiet. Say it, he thought, but gently, as gentle and wishful as he imagined his hand on her hair would be if he allowed it to reach for her. He knew that if he did, if he touched her, the thing she would say would not be, could not be, the thing he was waiting for her to say, which could not be a thing he drew from her, with even the gentlest touch.

Maude didn't say anything. The moon went on shining, the junk in the trees hung there, and Byron thought of how the moonlight made the white splotches on his cow's back glow, and of how simply cheerful all those men in the Rainbow had seemed.

So Byron Doatze shifted slowly into reverse and half turned toward her so that he could see out the back window. He met her eyes, and saw how sad and steady they were, and how set her mouth was, the strong line of her jaw. He kept one hand on the wheel and the other on the back of the seat, and he said. "He stood up like a man would. He still had his hand in the back of the dummy, and then he pulled his hand out, so gently, and held the dummy out to me."

She nodded then, and he saw her mouth soften, and to keep from doing anything else, to keep from having to decide what that meant, he looked behind the truck and started backing up, his eyes on the wagon track that was washed red by his backup lights.

They rode the two miles to the edge of town in the silence of the truck's tires and the truck's motor and the knowledge of breathing. As they passed the first houses, Byron tried to remember if he'd held the boy's hand or not. But even as he was thinking it, he knew he was wondering about it so that he wouldn't be waiting to hear what she said, wondering if she'd say anything at all.

They were pulling up in front of her house before she cleared her throat quietly and said, "You should have been honored."

For just a second a smoothness appeared in Byron's mind, a simple smooth area, and then he said, "Yes. I guess I should have been. But I wasn't. I gave it to Nobel, and he carried it back." The words came out easy and surprised in spite of how the thing he could only call his heart rose up almost to his throat, so full and grateful that it should have choked him.

She didn't say anything else, and neither did he. He was waiting again now, but for something—for *what* it would be, not *if* it would be. So when he had pulled on the brake, and she had opened the door, and she reached to gather her books from the seat between them, Byron took her wrist gently and raised her hand and kissed her palm as if it was a thing that could be done, knowing the scent and taste of this woman's curved palm as he let her warm wrist slide free of his loose grasp. As if it was possible, she touched his face, her cool fingers briefly across his cheek, beside his eye, and then carefully, delicately, across his lips.

Neither of them said anything else, not even good night, as she stepped down from the truck, but he watched her walk to her door, the moonlight picking out those flowers on her full skirt, and when she paused there, and then turned and raised her hand, he raised his too, and then he waited while she went in, waited until he saw her kitchen light come on, before he drove on home, not even thinking, not even hearing himself whistling softly over the steady hum of his engine.

Running Out

THESE DAYS MIKE accepted the small pleasures that came to him. He was pleased when the last bag of rubbish from inside exactly filled the outside garbage can on the morning Old Will came by on his dump run. The pleasure didn't last, of course. Even a man in Mike's circumstances, unemployed and unexpectedly without his wife, couldn't find deep pleasure in such accidental perfections. A deep pleasure would be, maybe, coming home tonight from somewhere and smelling spaghetti sauce as he got to the front door, hoping, and then scorning himself for hoping, and then hoping again, and getting inside to find Vicky truly home. The moment when she turned around in the kitchen and spoke to him, as if she'd never been gone—he tried sometimes to figure out what she should say to make it perfect, but he hadn't hit it yet—that, *that* would be a deep pleasure. In the meantime, he took what he could: filling one garbage can level in exactly seven days, going down to the cellar with the right number of hangers just as the dryer stopped, folding a slice of Swiss cheese to match the size of a slice of bread. If he'd been counting, he could have added up a good number of these small things by the time he put that trash beside the driveway. But he wasn't a counter, even if he sensed the weight of sunshine floating in as he woke, a perfect shave, and his shirt tucking in right the first time.

HE WALKED into the diner at exactly ten o'clock and called out, "Hey, Nancy! Where's my coffee?" He liked calling out, as he used to like calling Vicky "woman" in their kitchen.

The diner was about half full, maybe a dozen people, three couples in booths, a few people at the counter. Mike knew all but one couple by face or name. The number was just right: any fewer and Nancy and Mary would talk to him about not having a job, or about Vicky leaving him. That was such a beating, either way, that on days when nobody was there but Jim Parsons at one end of the counter, with his little tin teapot, and some traveling family at a booth, Mike would order his coffee to go, and look through jukebox titles while he waited.

Mary seemed to think she was an employment agency, and she'd offer to mention his name to bosses who came in for coffee. Terrific. Mike's life was built of certain simple facts that Mary, balloon boobs and brain to match, couldn't seem to get a firm hold on. Mike knew how to do what he did: finish carpentry. And he didn't do anything else; he did woodwork, trim, especially restoration, any kind of finish work. And that's all. He *could* take a job washing dishes, or delivering dry cleaning for the place in Slaters Falls. He could do some kind of dull work for eight hours a day and not make any more than he got on unemployment. But one of these days, probably before his unemployment ran out, somebody around Clayborne or up in Livingston or someplace was going to need a finish man, and he'd be all set. In the meantime—thank you, Mary.

Nancy was smarter by twenty miles than Mary, but she had this thing about him and Vicky that wouldn't quit. She'd gone to school with Vicky, though they hadn't been particular friends, and she thought she had some kind of right. The first couple of times she had started in on it he'd tried to change the subject, but then he'd gotten teed off. "What are you, writin' a book?" he had snarled, so mad he'd left without paying for the coffee. He hadn't gotten a chance to drink it, why the hell should he pay for it? Let her drink the goddamn coffee. The next morning the diner was busy. He didn't have a thing to say to her anyway. But by the next day he had let it go, and everything was fine for about a week, until she had time to come and lean her hip against the counter in front of him. Two sentences, and she was at it again, like it was a project.

"Look, Nancy," he'd said, "just forget it. It's no big deal, happens all the time. I'm fine, she's fine. No big deal."

"Okay, sure, but sometimes talking about it helps, you know?"

"Helps what, for crying out loud?"

She had turned a little toward him, rolling that hip along the counter edge. "Come on! You don't just forget it, you know—it eats at you, and if you can get it out . . ."

"Nancy, there ain't no *it*! No eat, no it, no out, no nothing!"

"You're such a big strong man you don't even notice Vicky's not there in bed anymore?"

"What, you get a mail-order shrink diploma?"

"Doesn't take a shrink to see you're sore and lonely."

"Look, don't get confused—you think I come in here because I'm lonely? You really think if I was lonely I'd be spending time in *here*, talking to *you*?"

"Okay." She had taken her cigarettes out of her uniform pocket, from under the apron, and lit one, staring off down the empty counter. "Okay." She exhaled. "So. Think it'll stop raining?"

"Always does," he'd said. Caught between satisfaction and shame, he'd left her a dollar tip. After that, if she looked like she wanted to talk, he just ordered his coffee to go.

But today was perfect: just enough people, not too busy.

"Hey, Nancy! Where's my coffee?" He took his regular place, between the doughnuts and the eternal layer cake. She came out of the kitchen and stopped dead, like he was the last person she ever expected to see in the spot he had filled every morning for six weeks.

"Where's that other guy?" she said.

Mike looked over his shoulder. "What other guy?"

"The guy who was sitting there a minute ago."

"In *my* place?"

"Yeah, just a minute ago."

"Oh, him—that big guy?"

"Yeah, big guy sitting right there. Ordered coffee."

"Big guy, bald, leather jacket?"

Nancy nodded, holding back a grin.

"Big chain around his neck? Little monkey on the stool next to him, holding the chain?"

"Right, that's him! Where'd he go?"

Mike shrugged. "Dunno—he was gone when I got here."

Nancy laughed, congratulating him. "Guess you'll have to drink his coffee, then," she said.

And then she poured his coffee and brought it to him. It was fresh, it was hot and black, it smelled like Sunday morning from upstairs. She put the cup down in front of him, slid over a lidded pitcher of cream, and went off down the counter. Mike poured a thin stream of white from the metal pitcher, and it dove down through the coffee and curled back up. He stirred, and the coffee took the color of old oak woodwork, a color luminous and solemn. He sipped cautiously: it was coffee like no coffee had been, or could be again. He raised the cup a second time and smelled deeply before he drank. That coffee was flavor and comfort, pure warmth, pure pleasure, coffee blessed and bestowed upon him. Perfection in a thick white cup.

He drank it as slowly as he dared, wanting it to last forever, fearing it would begin to cool.

When it was gone, he held the cup for a moment in both hands. Nancy went by, writing on her pad as she walked. Many days he just stayed in the diner until the lunch crowd started coming in, nursed two or three cups of coffee, talked about nothing with people he knew, joked around with Nancy, and bought the paper to read at home with his lunch. But today—well, there wasn't going to be another cup of coffee like that one, and the weather was too good to waste. The sunshine coming down warm through a thin breeze on his way in was still out there; in here he felt like he'd had the best of it already. He put the heavy cup down on the counter and left two quarters beside it. Jim Parsons came in and said, "You leaving already, Mike? I must be running late."

"Either that or I'm ahead of myself," Mike said. They shook hands, and Mike went to pay Mary at the cash register. The out-of-town couple from the front booth came right behind him, so Mary didn't even get to ask if he'd found anything yet, and Mike got the pleasure of making her blush by grabbing and kissing her hand when she held it out to take his dollar bill. They both laughed, and Mary said, "Why, *Mis*ter Connor!" But that blush was fine, right down her throat into the V of her uniform. Mike pressed the dollar bill into her hand.

"You have a *good* day, sweetheart," he said, his voice deep with mock passion. He patted her shoulder and went out the door without waiting for his change.

AFTER BEING in the sun, Mike had trouble seeing inside the dim post office, but he could see through the little glass door of his box that at least the top envelope was a letter. He turned the brass knob through the combination, heard the miniature weights of the cylinder drop, and pulled out three envelopes.

Helen, behind the counter, didn't even look up from her ledger as he walked back over the dull old floorboards and out the door. Helen was Vicky's aunt, and she hadn't spoken a civil word to him in four months, since the end of his last job. She did, however, usually speak. "Man of leisure," she'd say, or "Must be nice," or just "Some people," with disgust in her voice as dark and thick as the hair over her lip. Helen made getting the mail, Mike had said to Vicky, like going to a VD clinic. And Vicky had laughed at him, back in the winter, laughed and said, "Oh, Mike, you know she does everybody that way—even me." He'd made Vicky go with him the next day, to see if she was right.

"Morning, Aunt Helen," Vicky had said. "Beautiful day out there!"

"For those who can be out there," Helen had said back, and sniffed.

He'd felt Vicky barely keeping back her whoopy laughter; all the way home she'd held on to his arm, laughing. "Did you see how she wrinkles her nose when she sniffs? Makes you worry about that moustache, you know? One day it'll go right up!"

But things hadn't stayed that way. They'd been married a year before he got laid off, and though his being out of work hadn't changed the money that much, something, some way of not having a job, he didn't seem to be able to figure out. He was home too much, or out too much, or something. One morning he got home with the mail and said to Vicky, "Your aunt was really sweet today—she took the time to inform me that I'm still around."

"So?" No smile.

"Nice of her to notice, don't you think?"

"Pretty hard not to, isn't it." Not a question. End of conversation. He'd left the mail on the table and gone back out.

So Helen's ignoring him today was one more pleasure, and he didn't hang around to see if it would last. He took his mail out into the sun at the foot of the post office steps. One letter was from his mother, addressed, in defiance, to Mr. and Mrs.; another was from the Electric and Gas; the third was a letter with no return address—probably junk. He could go back to the diner to open them. He looked that way, remembering that cup of coffee but already knowing how disappointing another would be, and the lunch crowd would be coming in. Then he saw Vicky's oldest brother, Ben.

"Ben," Mike said.

Ben nodded, said "Mike," and put out his hand.

"Good to see you," Mike said, grateful for the simple warmth of the older man's dry hand.

"Been out of town," Ben said. "You working yet?"

"Nope, still waiting."

"Nice weather for it."

"Nice weather for working, too."

They both smiled. "I heard something about Tony Andrellos getting a crew together for some job—train depot or something," Ben said.

"Oh, yeah? Maybe I'll give him a call. Thanks."

"I don't know how solid it is. Just something I heard."

"Okay—I'll give him a call."

"Well," Ben said.

"Yup," Mike said. It was the moment when Ben might say something about Vicky, so, as much as he liked Ben, liked standing here in the sun with him, he said, "I better get along. Good to see you, Ben."

"You too."

Mike turned and headed home. He hated to go in out of this sunshine, so he sat on his front steps to open his mail. Electric and Gas. A check. Seventy-five dollars, payable to Michael R. Connor, refund of deposit. He grinned. Free money, no doubt about it. Made him feel so good, along with seeing Ben that way and the sunshine and all, he almost didn't want to open his mother's letter. But he folded the stiff check to fit exactly into his shirt pocket and tore open his mother's envelope.

She'd sent a note folded around a newspaper clipping. "Dear Mike and Vicky, Just thought you might get a kick out of this. Love,

Mom." The clipping was from the *Livingston Weekly* and included two pictures of the Livingston Hotel, before and after restoration. The headline read, LOCAL LANDMARK REDEDICATED, and the article reported that Mike Connor, son of Mr. and Mrs. Richard Connor, of Boyd Street, Livingston, and graduate of Livingston High, married to the former Victoria Spencer, daughter of Mrs. Wanda Spencer and the late Randall Spencer, of Clayborne, had worked on the restoration. Mike chuckled, knowing this was the kick his mother meant—the *Weekly* and its way of working as many local families as possible into every story—and he winced just the least bit, wondering if whoever wrote the article knew about Vicky leaving him. But even with all that, he was glad to have the pictures.

The old hotel had been his last job, good work, good crew, good money. He'd spent three weeks just on the banister of the stairway, and nobody had tried to make him hurry or fake it or anything. Somebody had tried to gild the mahogany rail somewhere along the line. He'd done the stripping and the refinishing and the replacements for the spindles; even he would have trouble now saying which of the spindles were original and which were his. He slipped the clipping and note back into the envelope. He took the third envelope, unopened, in with the other two, and put them all on the table while he made his lunch.

He'd made his sandwich, folding the cheese and meat to fit the bread, and poured himself a glass of milk, when the phone rang.

"What the hell you doin' in the house on a day like this?" It was Jerry.

"What the hell you doin' talkin' obscenities over the phone lines?"

"Just tryin' to save my buddy from gettin' rickets from lack of sunshine."

Mike laughed because he knew what was coming, and Jerry came through, tidy as can be: "Now, we all know that for rickets you got to have two things: exercise and yeast. And over at the Inn they got some nice cold yeast and a nice green exercise machine. How about it, Mikey? Shoot some eight ball?"

"You know me, Jerry—anything for my health. Meet you there in half an hour, okay?"

"You got any bread?"

"How much you need?"

"Oh, five bucks, somethin' like that."

"Man, I'm wealthy today—got this refund. No problem."

"Well, then, we got us a game!"

Mike hung up and went back to the table, where that last envelope was sticking out from under the other two. Why not, he thought, and opened it. Though his address had been typed, the letter inside was handwritten and short:

> Mike,
> My bus gets in to Slaters Falls at 7:30
> Wednesday night. Can you meet me?
> Vicky

He read it twice, to be sure, but there it was, better than he could have imagined or planned it. She was coming, whether or not, and asking only if he'd be there, but asking it, and with just enough time between his knowing and his getting there tomorrow night. When she got off the bus, she'd have to be glad to see him, just because he had come as she asked. And they couldn't even start trying to explain or settle anything there in public, so the first few minutes, at least, would be friendly and easy. And then the twenty-minute ride home alone in the simplicity of the car. Or more than twenty minutes, if they wanted to take it, if they were talking and they needed to go on longer; they could keep riding around like they used to when they never seemed to have enough time alone together. He smoothed the letter out on the table.

THE DOOR of the Inn was propped open with a broken bar stool, and Jerry was alone at the bar sipping a draft when Mike got there. He heard the delicate rattle of balls from the back room.

"Competition?" he asked, tipping his head toward the poolroom.

"Kids," Jerry said. "Broke kids. They'll be done in about"—he raised his half-empty glass like a gauge—"twelve ounces."

"Sounds good. Hey, Charlie!"

Fat Charlie looked up from his paper behind the bar.

"You called?"

"Eight ball in the side pocket. Cash a check?"

"How big?"

"Seventy-five."

Charlie swiveled on his stool and rang the register open, ruffled through the bills inside. "No problem. Personal?"

Mike signed the check and slid it across the bar. "No problem, Charlie, like you said. This one's backed by God Almighty. And gimme a Pabst out of that and two bucks in quarters, and a drink for my buddy here."

Charlie set the beers on the bar and the pile of bills beside them, with the quarters on top in two equal stacks. Mike felt under the end of the one for the end of a ten, took it between his thumb and forefinger, and pulled it sharply. It came out the way a magician's tablecloth comes from under the china. Jerry whistled his admiration, and Mike presented him with the ten, a dry flourish in the air.

"I don't know, buddy—looks like you're hot today. Maybe I better stay off that table."

"Have no fear, have no fear. Flip for the break?"

"I call."

Mike tossed a quarter in the air.

"Heads," Jerry said. He caught the quarter and slapped it onto the bar. "Tails it is. The man's on a roll."

"Then let's get in there before you put so much mouth on it it's gone."

Jerry grinned at Charlie. "Sore winner," he said, and followed Mike into the back room, where the two kids were just leaving.

Mike made the six on the break, a good scattered break that left him three pretty good shots. He made them all. Then he made the seven ball, not so easy, but clean. Jerry, leaning against the wall, started chalking his cue. The cue ball was right against the rail; Mike's only shot was a probable scratch on the five. He stepped back from the table, looking for an angle, and then stepped up and shot. The five dropped, and the cue bounced softly off the pocket corner, a fraction this side of a scratch.

"Nice shot," Jerry said.

The three ball looked impossible, so Mike chalked quickly and tried a three-rail shot, in total confidence that he'd miss but leave Jerry a tough start. The cue ball caromed crazily, nicked the three, and sent it, slow as oil on a puddle, into the pocket. Mike stared. Jerry hooted and came over to the table to slap him on the back.

"What the hell kind of shot was that?"

Mike shook his head, grinning.

"*Hooh!* I'd have bet you your whole ten bucks you wouldn't make that shot in a million years!" Jerry was tickled. He was beside Mike now, the two of them competing together against the table. They both looked at the eight ball, hugging the rail near a corner but apparently closed in on two sides by all the stripes.

"It's not makable," Mike said.

"Neither was that last one, buddy," Jerry said. He walked around to the end of the table and squatted to get his eye at ball level. "Come here, Mike—here, look at this. If you just stroke it in like that, just impulse it through right there—"

"No way, man."

"What do you mean, no way? Get over here and look at it." Mike went over. Jerry squinted at the shot. "You just want to *push* the cue ball through, see?"

"Jerry, that ball's not going through there unless I shrink it, and I didn't bring my magic shrinking powder."

Jerry aimed his squint up at Mike. "You don't want to try to run it out, or what? Hunker down here and *look,* big shot."

Mike hunkered down and looked, and he saw it: just barely, from there, Jerry might be right. The shot was, in theory, barely makable. "Okay," he said, and stood, and Jerry moved out of the way, and Mike shot.

"Oh, too *hard,* man!" Jerry groaned, as the cue hit the ball. But he was wrong. The white ball stalled when it hit the eight, and the eight, as if it had an acre of clear green felt to play on, rolled clean out of the forest of stripes and plunked calmly into the corner pocket.

"I don't believe it!" Jerry yelled. "Holy shit, Mike—I mean you are *hot* today! I thought you blew it, I really thought you blew it, and there it goes—damn!"

Mike was still looking at the table, trying to see how it had happened. He knew he'd hit the cue ball too hard, at least for the shot he'd been trying to make. It made him feel funny, just for a second, and then Jerry shook his shoulder, slapped his back.

"Hey, Fats! Come on, come on, my turn. You rack 'em up, and Jerry gets a shot."

Mike laughed. He hadn't run the table in years, not since high school, when he used to go to the old Livingston Hotel every day after school and shoot.

Jerry got his shot. On the break he got the eleven, and then missed sinking the twelve by a hair. Mike looked the table over carefully, planned out the next two shots, while Jerry ragged him. "What's hot gets cold, man, and what's cold warms up, don't forget. You can't last forever, just remember that, buddy."

Mike grinned at him and pointed with his stick. "One ball, corner pocket," he said. And ran the table again. Charlie came back to watch it, and he and Jerry said less and less, just a low whistle now and then after a pretty shot. This time the eight was easy, but they all watched it in silence anyway, and stared at the pocket as the ball rattled into the rack below.

Jerry racked for Mike's break. The two and the ten dropped, and Mike looked at the table for a long time before deciding. "Three in the side," he said.

And ran the table again, easing the eight in more gently, more hopefully, than he had ever done anything in his life.

"Phenomenal, man," Jerry said. He'd stood his cue against the wall three shots ago, and didn't move now from where he leaned beside it. "Phenomenal. We should take you on tour."

"I don't know if I ever saw that before," Charlie said, as quiet as Jerry. "Three runs in a row like that."

Mike laid his stick across the table. "What the hell time is it anyway?"

"Four-thirty."

"Time for a beer," Mike said.

"You don't want to start fuzzing up when you're shooting like that," Jerry said.

"I'm done shooting. Now I'm drinking."

"Done?"

Mike laughed. "Yeah—had my exercise, now I want my yeast."

They went out to the bar, and Jerry slapped Mike's shoulder again. "Well, I called it, boy—you are hot."

"I was hot, Jer, and now I'm thirsty."

"Thirsty? You had a beer, not three hours ago—what's this thirsty?"

"Yeah, I had it, but I didn't get to drink it. You're one lazy pool player, man."

"You hear that, Charlie? Here I am, keeping up this billiard hall so the great man can perform, and he calls me names."

The beer Charlie set in front of Mike, and refused to take money for, was so cold it frosted the glass to the top. Mike raised his glass to Jerry, a salute of gratitude, and Jerry raised his in return. Then Mike drank, and the beer, gold and cold, was as fine as the morning's thin breeze had been.

AT SIX O'CLOCK Mike unlocked his kitchen door and let himself in. Vicky's letter lay in the center of the table; it had folded itself partway back up. He looked at it for a second, but he didn't want to read it again. Just that it had come should be enough. Just that she was coming back, whatever that was going to mean. He went to the refrigerator, pulled out the package of sliced ham, and ate the two pieces that were left. He looked in the refrigerator again. He was nearly out of a lot of things—milk, butter, one egg left. Maybe he should go over to the store and stock up before Vicky got back.

But not tonight. He went to the door of the living room, still thinking about that last eight ball, how generously it had moved for him. And now the light came slanting into the living room, and, as Mike watched, the rectangle of sun on the floor stretched an inch, two inches, and for a sudden moment it matched exactly the size and shape of the living room carpet. Some slight cloud must have moved out of the way just then, for the light pulsed stronger. Mike stood for a few seconds there, pleased at the exactness of it. Before the light could change again, begin to fade, he turned and went back through the kitchen and up the stairs.

He inspected the bathroom and the bedroom, thinking maybe he'd do some cleaning before getting Vicky tomorrow, but he couldn't see much to do. He'd had so little to do the past few weeks, he'd spent a lot of the time organizing and cleaning in the house, just to keep busy.

He went back down and out, heading to the diner for supper. This would be the last diner supper for a while, he reminded himself. But right now, right now, halfway between his front steps and the front door of the diner, everything was exactly perfect. For just a moment he was fully, deeply pleased. A breeze came up, the smell of daffodils from somewhere, that sad sweet smell. How nothing perfect lasted.

He decided against the diner, in favor of walking. Just keep walking for a while. If he could have found a way, an easy way, well this side of death, to keep everything just as it was forever, he'd have taken it. Any minute of today, he'd have taken it. Drink that one cup of coffee all damn day if he could. Couldn't. Vicky'd be home, tomorrow.

The Snake

THE BELT OF somebody's bathrobe lay in a dark heap in the middle of the kitchen floor. Never mind that nobody had a bathrobe any more, that all the belts and bathrobes had burned to ash, along with my marriage and what I had imagined my life to be, three weeks ago and three miles away. When I stepped into the trailer, I had two bags of groceries in my arms, my children were coming across the yard with three more, I needed to get water on to boil for noodles if we were going to get supper fixed and eaten by bedtime, and, by the way, somebody had left the belt of a bathrobe lying on the kitchen floor. So I put the first bag on the counter beside the stove, flipped on the overhead light, the belt seethed and rose up knee-high and hissing, and here I was, outside, empty-handed, at the far end of the yard, knees and elbows jerking like a puppet's, with my plan for water boiling in the saucepan a shining metal button holding the center of my mind.

Dusk was coming on. Before long now darkness would begin to gather under the trees and wild bushes that surrounded the yard, and the coarse patchy grass would look soft and fine for a few minutes before it disappeared into night. I knew I had to get done with this wild breathless marching, and finish with the boasting I hadn't even started yet, and get on with what had to be done. Pretty soon now I'd have to start talking, and then stop talking, and cross the yard, pass my rigid children, pull that trailer door open, and, somehow, dispose of the snake. I would have to do it because there was no one else to do it, because I was the only hero here. Any minute now, that was going to have to start happening.

Miriam must have known that. She turned fiercely to the younger two. "Shut up and sit down," she said. She was ten, and had certain privileges and duties, especially since I had driven their father away. Kimberly and Jonah, who admired her, as did I, sat down where they were, cross-legged on the damp ground with their grocery bags in their laps. "And stay there," Miriam said. "You can eat some of those oyster crackers."

I turned at the corner of the yard and crossed again, the longer grass catching at my ankles as I paced, waiting for my joints to reclaim their strength.

After a long moment of rattling, Kimberly said, "We can't get the bag open."

Miriam turned and bent to open the bag at the very moment I stopped marching and said I was acquainted with snakes, and so my words must have hit her like an accusation, from behind.

"I am acquainted with snakes," I said. I never meant it for Miriam. I said it across the yard, said it past the children and through the wall of the trailer, aiming only for the snake.

"I am familiar with snakes; all my life I have lived where snakes lived; this is nothing new to me, let me tell you," I said. "I once watched my mother chop a snake up in the driveway with a hoe," I said.

The snake, dodging across the kitchen in mad angles, did not hear, was not warned.

Miriam did, was.

"What's she going to do?" Kimberly said.

"I don't know," Miriam said.

Jonah sighed, licking the salt off the little round crackers.

"Will—"

"Shut up," Miriam said. "Just shut up."

But I wasn't finished yet. I heard the children, but I had my boasting to do, my stories to remember so I'd be able to go back in there. I folded my arms across my chest and spoke louder. "My grandmother beat a snake to death with a mop handle on the milkroom floor when she was sixteen—I know what I'm talking about," I said. "A snake came right into my father's sickroom when he was dying, and he threw a blanket over it and called the dog and the dog came and killed it. My Uncle Warren shot eight snakes in one afternoon when he was looking for a lost cow, and he nailed them all to the side of the barn."

All this was true, and more: how the snakes had used to come swarming up out of the cistern while the men were filling it, rippling smooth and steady up over the lip and then disappearing, as if they had melted into the ground; the short green snakes my brother had chased me with; the bull snake that had dropped like a heavy length of black hose right over the door of Aunt Ann's house one Easter morning and flowed under the foundation before our very eyes. I knew all this, and I knew about Don't Tread on Me, the Garden of Eden, Freud, narrow fellows in the grass, mythical hoop snakes, the caduceus; I knew about forked tongues and Medusa.

I knew it all and I remembered it, but all that was long ago and far away, longer and farther than even three weeks and three miles. I hadn't seen a single snake in my adult life. Maybe the simple absence of snakes had allowed me to live that dozen years, snuggling my babies and stirring my stews and weaving small beautiful baskets and keeping in careful love with my husband, without ever having had to be a hero. Maybe if I'd seen a snake or two I'd have seen, too, that my life was so achieved, so unnaturally good, and thus so vulnerable to the least wrong gesture, that to be safe I should never have snuggled or stirred or loved or walked like a free woman among the grasses of the fields.

But in the real life before that false peaceful one, there had been snakes, and now, even from way at the back of the yard, I could hear the one in my kitchen, the dry muscular rustle and slither of its scales across the floor. So I said it, said, "I know how to deal with a snake."

"My brother," I said, but by now I was almost ready. I didn't look at the children but I knew they were there, and I knew I hadn't betrayed them, wouldn't betray them (as their father had and over such a small thing, such a silly thing—I think it was the first time I had dared or needed to think the word "betray"). They needed their supper, they had school tomorrow, and so I began thinking of tools, weapons, a rusty tire iron I'd seen somewhere, the remains of a fallen swing set. "My brother used to catch snakes and whip them around the barbed-wire fence, and their skin would rip open, and their guts would go flying. We had a cat that killed a snake a week; there's no great problem with killing snakes," I said, and now I meant the children to hear, and I thought of saying that I myself once stepped barefoot on a snake behind the slide in my own backyard, which was true—I could still feel, when I thought of it, the cool surprising surge against my sole—but not a useful thing, just now. I had, in fact, never killed a snake. "I come from a long line of snake killers," I said instead.

Only three weeks had passed since the fire, and we had moved just three miles, but I had become a woman whose children wore white T-shirts and blue shorts and brown thongs every day because everything else was ashes and the insurance company was in no hurry. Three weeks had passed since their father walked away in his hurt pride, three weeks since I'd seen his face or heard his voice. For three weeks I'd been deciding one small thing after another, waiting for him to remember what a father was, what a husband was, even if his house had burned down and even if his wife didn't love him like his mother did, and this was what I had brought my children to, a borrowed trailer so ragged that snakes didn't know it was a home and came right in. I will vomit, I thought, imagining my hand on the doorknob, my feet on the wobbly wooden steps, imagining the rust of the tire iron stinging my palm. "Miriam," I called.

MIRIAM HAD BEEN the first one awake, lying, I imagine, for a puzzled moment, listening, before she ran to our room and said, "Daddy, the house is on fire." There had been sleep, dreams, and then, at once and everywhere in the house, each of us hurrying the others, abandoning quick searches in the dark, speaking clear, quiet words—Get Jonah, Hurry now, I have my shoes, Get out first, Here, Go down the back stairs, Don't trip on that, The cat's outside, We don't have time, I'll call from the Fosters', Hold Kimberly's hand—voices as hushed as if the fire were a monster not to be provoked. And then we were all outside, at the end of the driveway, as the fire came writhing up the back of the house. We watched Ty in his boxer shorts running barefoot down the slope, down the half mile to wake the nearest neighbors in the middle of the soft spring night to call the fire department, long after too late, which I knew, standing there, looking for the stars after I couldn't see Ty any longer, and which Ty knew, sweat itching his back as he banged and called at the Fosters' door.

The door wasn't even locked. He said that when he came back, breathing hard. "I should have just gone in the damned door," he said. "Too goddamned late now."

"It wouldn't have mattered," I said, to comfort him. He had nowhere to put his hands, and I wished Jonah were still small enough to need holding, wanted to give him Jonah to hold, just for that. If the children had cried, it would have been so different, but the only noise was the fire rushing wild through the house, as oddly peaceful as the sound of the children breathing in their sleep. I looked around for Miriam: I remember thinking she was the one who could step up to her father and take his hand, and then I heard the sirens far off, and then a small explosion inside the house.

The windows were full of the fire, the night was bright with the smoke, and I couldn't take my eyes from the house. I kept thinking of the things inside, little cherished things leaping up in my mind to be loved—oh, the green lamp, oh, my quilts, oh, the baby clothes in the plastic bags and now I'd never get them put into little round-topped trunks, oh, the yarn in oh, the blanket chest, oh, Miriam's library books, my basket weeds hung to dry in the kitchen, the undone ironing in the living room. And I was trying at the same time to remember that things don't matter.

The fire trucks turned onto our road, and we could see their lights flashing, the headlights of other cars coming behind. "At least we're all out safely," I said. "We can get another house."

"When?" Miriam said.

The fire trucks pulled into the yard too slowly, and the men climbed down carelessly in their big rubber boots as cars started arriving. I told the children to stay right there with me, out of the way. Ty ran to the men, who shook their heads and gestured. I couldn't make out in the light from headlights and the fire just who he was talking to, but it was clear they were sending him back out of their way. I was watching him arguing, and so I missed the moment the house sighed and fell.

When dawn came, the volunteers were emptying the last water-heavy hose at the smoking ashes; Ty stood behind them, the first light showing his tense spine up the center of his narrow bare back, his hands still empty at his sides. The dawn was beautiful, lavender and gray and rose along the horizon, and the Fosters' meadow looked like I imagine England, lush and glowing. The children were half asleep on the grass, leaning against one another like a pile of puppies. My brother had been among the volunteers earlier, and he had offered us the use of his old trailer until we decided what to do next. For a moment, there with day coming and the least mist rising from the fields, I felt a kind of euphoria: along with the house we'd lost everything the house had meant—the shape of our lives, the limits of it. We could do anything now. We could go to England, we could build a log cabin, we could move to a city.

I wanted to tell Ty that. I wanted to show him that the loss was not important; I wanted him to see that his hands weren't empty, and not just because we were all out here on the grass, safe and tired. The volunteers were finishing up, taking off their raincoats and rolling up the hoses, talking to each other but not to Ty, moving around him without touching him. He looked from the back so lone, so thin and chilled, that I knew I couldn't tell him how delight was rising up in me. I remembered Jonah's blanket in the backseat of the car and I went and got it and stepped up behind my husband and put the small blanket over his bare shoulders.

I meant that blanket as a boxer's robe, a gladiator's cape, a hero's cloak. I meant to say that the fire was not a failure but a victory, over the ways our life had grown small and safe.

I did not mean, as I understood he thought I did when he twisted away, to tuck him up in the baby's blankie.

HE WAS FURIOUS. That's all that was in his face: no grief, no sadness, no worry, not even embarrassment, which must have been what I had caused by trying to comfort him in front of other people. All he had for me was fury, his nostrils tensed, his eyes hard. When he spoke his lips were held away from his teeth. I was so startled, so shocked, and my mind still working on how to say how exciting life was about to become, it took me several seconds to hear what he said—"You take the damned car"—and by then he was gone, climbing into Mike Connor's station wagon.

ONE WRONG GESTURE, after all those dangerous times when I had asked more or appreciated less than his widowed mother always had, and here I was on another damp lawn, a five-foot rat snake writhing and waiting in my kitchen, keeping my children from their supper and their beds, and Ty was off somewhere indulging in defeat. I'd left the car there. It was all we had left, but the keys were in the house. I heard Ty had gone back to his mother's house, where he knew I'd never follow him; if he knew where we were, how we were, it wasn't because I'd told him, or because he'd asked.

"She went in the bushes to pee," Kimberly said.

Now, I thought, while you're still mad, and so I came across the yard. "You children stay right there," I said. "There's a snake in the trailer, and I'm going to kill it." My children peeing in the bushes like savages, *my* children.

In the long grass behind the trailer, I found the pieces of rusty swing-set pipe. Only one of them was completely disconnected from the rest, and it was shorter but heavier than I'd remembered. I lifted it, hefted it, swung once at the ground, and went back around to the steps.

"With that stick," Kimberly said, "that's how."

I don't like to kill a rat snake, my mother had said, my mother who never cursed, but the son of a bitch hissed at me in my own driveway.

The son of a bitch. The wooden steps trembled as I went up. One of the things I hate about trailers is that the doors always open out. The snake could be waiting right there, ready to slide out over my feet, five feet of cool urgent muscle, while I shrieked and went mad before my children's eyes.

I banged the door twice with the pipe, denting the vinyl coating, and then I stepped down one step and pulled the door open. "You son of a bitch," I said, scanning the spilled cans and cartons.

Beyond them, the kitchen floor was blank.

"Hiss at me, will you," I said.

I couldn't see it anywhere, and so it was everywhere. I took a two-handed grip on the pipe and stepped up into the trailer. I kicked a can of soup with the side of my foot, sent it rolling into the living room, and then I saw the snake out of the corner of my eye, a dark line sidling down the pale linoleum of the hall.

Maybe the snake was responding to the cool air that came in through the open door, and maybe all he intended to do was turn around and make his way calmly to that open door, down the steps, and back to wherever last night's rainstorm had driven him out of. This is entirely possible, and, had I been thinking, I could have thought of it, and could have stepped quietly into the living room and stood on the seat of the saggy brown chair and watched him go, and then could have called to the children to make noise so he wouldn't go in their direction, and we'd have been rid of him just like that. Entirely possible.

I ran at him, yelling nothing. I slammed at him with the pipe, and got him somewhere in the middle of his back, and before he could even hiss I hit him again, and then he was a coiling mass, knotting and hooping up and around himself. The narrow hall was full of him, roiling and seething and thumping—he looked like hysterical screaming, like a mad black brain, and I didn't care about anything in the entire world but making him stop. I knew I should try to hit his head but I couldn't see where it was, I just clubbed at him again anywhere, and my hands were so sweaty the pipe flew and went skidding down the hall past the bathroom door. I stumbled through the groceries on the floor and grabbed the saucepan off the hook and ran back and beat at him with that. The noise was awful, the pan ringing and ringing when it hit the bare floor; he kept flailing and flopping; twice part of him slapped against my ankles, and then I could see his head, sleek and blunt, and his face: the black glitter of his eyes and his flat nostrils and that mouth, stretched back from the fangs, the paleness of it against the rest of him. I bent and aimed for that face with every blow. I hit him and hit him, and finally, finally, he stopped moving, and then I could hear how I sounded, and then I had to know that the children were out there in the dark hearing me, and I made myself drop the saucepan, and then I made myself stop the rest of it, the *ay-ay-ay-ay-ay*. The exulting.

I wanted to keep on yelling. I wanted to grab that snake by the thick tail and drag him outside and run around and around the trailer dragging him across the ragged grass and yelling. I could already imagine the weight of him; my palm wanted to feel if his flesh would still lurch or throb as I grasped it. Oh, I'd touch him now, I'd touch him all right—I'd swing him around my head in the dark! I'd dance with that five feet of broken slither, that undone writhing, that sidle gone limp—I'd dance my victory, I'd yell it to the night and make sure all the snakes in the bushes between the trailer and the river heard about it.

The snake's head was crushed and the skin behind it torn, but there was remarkably little blood—a streak on the floor, a few freckles of it on my hands and arms, a smear on the pan bottom. I heard my own breath rushing loud and clean in the air of the trailer. I felt my heart beating.

And then headlights swung across the wall, a car stopped outside, the car doors opened and shut, and Ty came bounding up the steps and into the trailer, like a hero to the rescue.

I wanted just a few more minutes, and I wanted it fiercely—to stand victorious over that snake, to call the children in to see that I had slain the dragon. I did want that. But Ty was sudden and beautiful, bounding in that way, his hair flowing, his eyes bright, the planes of his face new and fine to my eyes again. He smelled very young and clean. He looked at me and then at the groceries around his feet, and back at me. I wondered how I looked, and I was already pushing my wish for a wild victory dance into a shape that would wrap around Ty when the second car pulled up, and the third.

"Are you all right?" Ty said. He was looking at me, but he was listening to the car doors slamming.

"Yes," I said, and pointed to the snake.

"Damn," he said, and turned and went outside without looking at the snake at all.

I followed him, but I stopped on the steps when I saw the two men getting out of their cars—Danny Ward the town cop, and Jim

Parsons the minister. I saw Miriam standing beside Ty's car. And I saw then what had happened.

Miriam had run a quarter mile in her thongs to Byron Doatze's little stone house and used his telephone to call Ty. She had told him I had gone crazy.

Momma is marching up and down the yard in the coming-down dark shouting at the trailer, boasting about the murder of snakes, and the children are sitting in the grass eating crackers, and you have to come right now, Daddy, please.

Something like that, anyway, had happened, while I was doing what had to be done because I was the only one there to do it.

I thought I would never be able to look at her again.

I STOOD on the steps and my children stood on the grass. Ty hurried to meet the men, hands up to stop them, and then he shook his head, said, "False alarm," and gave a small laugh. Danny and Jim both sneaked a look at me before they laughed, uneasy. "She okay?" Danny said, and Ty laughed again, "She's fine—everything's under control."

And then they shook hands all around, as if they'd done something, and murmured things I couldn't quite hear. Then Ty said, "Thanks for coming," Danny said, "No problem, buddy," Jim said, "Any time you need me," both of them sort of backing up toward their cars.

"Good night," I called. I couldn't help it, I swear.

To their credit, they both called back, " 'Night," and Jim raised his hand as he pulled out and they both drove away, back toward town. It was full dark, and I watched their taillights for a long minute, thinking nothing at all.

"Can we go in now?" Kimberly said.

"Of course," I said. "It's getting late, and chilly. Come on, Jonah,

Miriam," I said. I went up the steps and into the kitchen, and they came after—Kimberly and then Jonah and then, with her face closed, Miriam, who left the door open.

The children paused inside, looking at the snake heaped in the hall. I started unloading the bag that still sat on the counter.

"You children want to gather up that stuff on the floor," I said. Miriam picked up two cans and handed them to Kimberly. "We'll get this cleaned up, and then I'll start some supper. You must be starving." Miriam brought the boxes of crackers and cereal into the kitchen and put them into the cupboard.

Ty came up the steps with the other three bags of groceries as I was putting the milk and juices in the refrigerator. He had to go by me to put the bags on the table, and by me again to get out of the kitchen. The young way he smelled was his mother's house, air freshener and warm plastic.

I shut the refrigerator. "You can pick up cans, too, Jonah," I said. Ty was watching them. "I thought I'd make noodles," I said, to anyone, and reached for the saucepan, which wasn't, of course, on its hook, but in the hall with the snake. Before I could take a step Miriam dodged past me and past her brother and sister and past Ty and grabbed the pan. Ty made a motion to touch her as she came back, but she twisted away from him and carried the bloody pan by the handle in both hands, as if it weighed twenty pounds, straight back to the kitchen, to the sink. She turned on the hot water and got out the dish soap and a steel wool pad and started scrubbing at the pan, her face completely blank.

I watched my daughter scouring at the snake's blood on the saucepan. She was only ten years old, and she had run through the dark to betray us all to save us all, and she knew what she had done and she was asking, now, no quarter.

I let her scrub the pan, and my heart filled with what she had meant: here we were, Ty in the living room with the children, me in the kitchen, supper about to be cooked. Miriam had done this, by herself, and now she was washing away the blood. And she was so young, with so long a time left to go.

But behind Ty in the living room with the children was the dead snake in the hall, the thing I had done, by myself.

I went into the living room and Ty moved to step in front of me. He said, "I'll get that," his voice low and careful.

"You will not," I said. I stopped and met his eyes.

Perhaps I had embarrassed him. Perhaps the loss of the house had unmanned him. Perhaps I should have needed him more. And perhaps, standing there considering his wish to dispose of the body of the beast, I should have considered all that, weighed what the children needed against what I needed, my sins against his, but all I was thinking was that the son of a bitch hissed at me in my own driveway.

"You will not," I said.

I went and got the snake. I bent down, wondering how heavy it was, and put my two hands around it, around the sticky flesh just behind the flattened head, and there was no throb to it, no jerk left. Ty said, "Addie?"

I just said, "Excuse me," backing up, dragging the snake at its full length through the living room and out the open door, down the uncertain steps, the snake thumping as it came down.

The yard was dark now, full dark. I didn't yell, and I didn't dance. This was real and necessary. I dragged the snake across the worn dirt and the clumps of rough grass, around back, out beyond the light that fell from the trailer. At the edge of the yard, just beyond the first bushes, the ground began to drop toward the river; the snake had probably come up from there, and I wanted to throw it back where it had come from. It was too long for me to gather up to throw, even if it hadn't been surprisingly heavy in death.

I took a good grip on it and began to turn around, dragging it in a circle around me. I turned faster, around and around; I spun in the dark until the snake rose up and I could let go, let it go flying out beyond the wild ragged bushes, down the slope toward the river.

I stood a moment, hearing its body slide and drop through the branches of the small bushes invisible below me. Then I went back into the trailer, leaving the door open behind me. Ty was standing in the living room. The younger two were there, too, by the window that looked out back.

Miriam was still in the kitchen. She had filled the clean saucepan with water and put it on the stove to heat. She had set the colander beside the sink, the bag of noodles on the counter. Her bangs were getting long.

Whatever blood I'd had on my hands had dried to an unpleasant feeling; whatever color it had been had mixed with the pipe rust. I had nothing to anoint my daughter with, and the time for such gestures, such confusions, was past. She was watching me carefully, so I nodded as I went to the sink. "Did you salt the water," I said.

She nodded, still watching me.

"Good girl," I said. I turned on the water and washed my hands. Over the sound of the water I said, "After we get the children to bed, we'd better take some of those newspapers and see if we can't stuff them around the pipes."

I don't know if Ty had watched me out the window. I don't know if he knew what I was doing. I don't know when he left.

The monster was dead, its body beginning to rot among the trees. "Kimberly, Jonah—better get that table set," I said. "You want to slice up a couple tomatoes, Miriam?" She opened the refrigerator. "And let's have some of that good cheese." I dried my hands on the dish towel. The water was beginning to boil. I tore open the bag of noodles.

Old Clayborne Trail

OLD CLAYBORNE TRAIL ran from the edge of the yard back into the woods. An abandoned road, weeds and grass grown up along its sides. A trail leading out, nothing, just a track into the woods, which perhaps were not deep woods, just leafy trees in summer, so close to the tire ruts that when Momma drove the car out the Trail the branches of the trees as well as the spindly undergrowth bushes grazed and swished and swabbed along the doors of the car, its roof, its windows. This was 1952, when cars still had starter buttons down among the pedals, and rounded hoods and roofs, and plush ropes slung across the backs of the front seats.

ONE EVENING, after the early supper, after everyone had gone back to the hayfields, trying for two, maybe three more loads before dark, Momma came out the back door and invited the children, the girl and the boy, to go with her for a ride in the car. She was learning to drive. For practice, she and Daddy sometimes went for a drive up the Trail, which started at the end of the yard and ran into the woods for a long way. They were living that summer with relatives of a sort, far out on a farm, and many days, like this one, no one at all was within two or three miles of the house except the children, who were three and four, and their mother, who was pregnant.

WHEN THE MOTHER came out the kitchen door that day, the girl was digging. If someone had asked her what she was doing, she would have said that. "Digging," she would have said. And later, the next night at supper, someone might ask where that tablespoon was, and say to the girl, "Were you playing with that spoon out back." The words would alarm her. She would think hurriedly about spoons and about out back. Unable to think about the fear the question caused, she would probably say no. She wouldn't intend to deny that she had been digging, or that she had spent long moments considering the spoon's bowl, and the flexibility of its handle. She was, maybe, a quieter child than some, less given to speaking. Maybe words alarmed her too easily, or tones of voices.

But if someone had asked her, kindly and simply, to describe her mother, had asked her to come and sit on the davenport and tell what her mother looked like, she would have tried. She would have come and sat where she was told to sit (recognizing directly from the adulthood of the asker that she was being told, not invited, no matter the exact words, the kindness of the tone), and she would have sat quietly, holding her hands in her lap, and her feet would have been busy, dangling that way, but she wouldn't have noticed that, would have thought she was quite still. And she would have tried to tell what her mother looked like.

"She has a round head," she would have said, speaking rather slowly, confidentially. "And hair." She might have raised her own hand then, the palm and back of it still plump, she was that nearly still a baby, might have raised her hand and held it near her own hair, only barely suspecting that the words might not describe her mother's hair. "She has two arms. With hands on them," and by then her brother would have come in to see what was going on in here, who the visitor was, and he might have stood quietly, because both of them were well behaved, and he was just a year older.

But his coming in, and some knowledge of her mother's hands, or maybe just the naming of the number two, might have distracted her enough that she'd have begun listing the facts she knew about bodies, how many eyes, and ears, how many fingers and toes, and maybe even that you see with your eyes and smell with your nose and hear with your ears. She might have considered, fleetingly, mentioning the belly button, since grownups seemed to be amused hearing of it, but, just as she had known the invitation to be an instruction, she would have known too that just now mention of the belly button would be inappropriate, unlikely to draw the pleased response. She would not have thought to mention her mother's actual belly button, or her mother's belly, huge as it was just then.

The boy might have mentioned it, though. He might have said, "And she has a great big stomach, as big as a balloon." He was that much older, in only a year.

And the fear would have been swift, low in her stomach, dark, and swift: that he'd be in trouble, that trouble would come of his having said.

THE CHILDREN were out back after supper. The boy was sitting in the swing, not swinging but turning around and around so the ropes twisted up and then twirled him down.

The girl was digging. She had found, already, the rusted screw-on cap from some small bottle, and two thick pieces of brown glass. The dirt was hard and dense. She pushed with the spoon, and the dirt broke away a little before the handle started to bend. The tip of the spoon's bowl went *tink* against something. She stopped, and turned the spoon around, and poked with the end of the handle, around and around the thing in the dirt that was hard. She put down the spoon and felt with her fingers, wiggled the thing and took it out, and rubbed at the dirt. Round and not round, smooth and then broken: a swirly marble, chipped on one side. The dirt squeaked between her fingers and the marble and pushed off in small clumps and flakes. A clear marble with red swirls inside. She waited, and then put the marble in the bowl of the spoon, where it rocked when she lifted the spoon. She poured the marble carefully into the old screw top; it fit exactly. She dug again, and then stopped, turned the marble in the small rusty cap so that the chipped side was down, invisible.

Their mother came out the kitchen door, and she said, "Would you like to go for a ride?" and because she was Momma and nobody else was there, the girl stayed squatting by the dirt she'd been digging, and the boy kept on twisting the swing for a good time before they both moved toward the car; it had not been a time of deciding but just of settling: the going for a ride, and Momma coming out and just exactly the way she was smiling, and Hugh and Connie and Daddy and even Deanna and Ray gone off haying, settling in among the digging and the twisting of the swing ropes. "Can Brownie come?" the boy said, and their mother said, "Yes."

THE GRASS growing up the middle of Old Clayborne Trail between the tire tracks so that if the car had been an animal the grass would have tickled its belly. The fat old dog with her head out the back window; the boy standing in the backseat, holding on to the plush rope; the girl riding in the front seat, the plush of the seat prickly against her bare legs; the mother and her belly behind the wheel, she working the key and pedals and the gearshift, and the car beginning to roll off across the yard for the Trail. For where it began, among the leafy, leafy trees. The mother as solemn now as the girl, the girl solemn, knowing from how the mother had smiled when she came out the kitchen door, or from some other exquisite thing for which she had also no words, that they might get in trouble for this, the girl keeping still.

It was summer, high summer, haying season, when people ate

early and went back out to the fields, when after supper spread on and on as if dark wouldn't come, high darkening summer in the broad farmlands, where abandoned roads ended at the edges of farmhouse yards.

THIS WAS NOT Eden. Old Clayborne Trail, going off among the trees for a long long way, Momma driving, shifting gears, going faster and shifting again where the trees fell back a bit and the Trail was straighter. In the armrest on the door, a metal ashtray with a lid that the girl raised carefully, waiting for the sudden pull of the spring at a certain point that snapped the lid full open and held it. Inside the ashtray, a small piece of crumpled cellophane and the torn wrapper of half a stick of gum, still scented with the gum, and with ashes. Far off, if they'd turned off the noise of the car, the sound of tractors. "Let's sing something," the boy said, and they didn't mind, so they sang something. They sang "Clementine," the girl feeling the sadness of "dreadful sorry, Clementine," even though the tune was happy. They sang "Jesus Wants Me for a Sunbeam," and "Jesus Loves Me This I Know," and "A Hole in the Bottom of the Sea"; they sang "Get Along Home, Cindy, Cindy," and the honeybees swarming around her mouth settled in with the worry the girl had had at the beginning. She closed the ashtray, slowly, and when the spring snapped the lid shut at the end, she didn't get pinched, and it made only the smallest click. The boy said, called, from the backseat where he stood on the floor behind the girl and held on to the plush rope like a cowboy on a bucking bronco, the boy called, "Do 'Apple Tree,' Momma," and Momma laughed. "Oh, the old apple tree in the orchard," she sang, "lives in my meh-hem-o-ree, for it reminds me of my pappy, he was handsome young and happy, when he died on the old apple tree." It was a bouncy song, the boy bounced in the backseat, the girl clapped along as Momma sang.

MAYBE IT WAS Eden. Maybe it was the time of their lives. Just them, riding along in the car on the road where nobody was, away from the house where too many people lived and the children were well behaved. The trees, the leaves, the apple tree song: "If my pappy had a knowed it, he'd be sorry that he growed it, for he died on the old apple tree." If only the girl hadn't had the fear coming in her stomach, trying not to notice how light was moving up and away from the green leaves all around, how color was moving off and away, and the darkness rising up.

Momma slowed down after the apple tree song. "I guess I'd bet-ter find a place to turn around," she said, and the girl was relieved that her mother had seen the darkness beginning, but the fear stayed as Momma made the car go slower and watched the sides of the Trail for a place to turn around. The girl watched, too.

The trees grew so close to the sides of the car, trees behind trees behind trees.

"Well, I'll try it up there," Momma said. "They'll be getting home soon."

They. Daddy, Hugh and Connie, Deanna and Ray. They lived that summer with Daddy's stepdaughter Connie from his previous marriage, with her husband Hugh, and their children. Momma and the girl and the boy, Daddy, Connie and Hugh, Deanna and Ray. Relatives of a sort, in a small farmhouse. Hugh said he could pick that kitchen table up with one hand and throw it out the door, and the girl believed that, but she wondered what would happen before he did it. Hugh's face looked like the face of a doll when you push back hard just beside the eyes. Once Connie shot a deer from the front porch early in the morning, but that was before they lived here. Deanna and Ray had chores. The girl didn't think of Daddy, had no picture or story to think of Daddy with.

———

WHEN THE car sound first stopped, the woods sounded silent. The car was turned sideways on the road. If another car came along it would smash into their car sideways on the road. The girl could think of that, but she could not think of the simple fact that they had never known any car but theirs to travel Old Clayborne Trail.

"I've stalled it," Momma said. When she looked around behind her, her hair swung back from her face. "All right," she said. She worked the shifting lever and looked down at her feet, at the pedals and at the round starter button. "All right," she said. "Here goes." She did with her feet and with the key. "It sounds like it has a bellyache," the boy said. Momma laughed. She did with her feet and the key again. "A really bad bellyache," the boy said. The girl watched the key, seeing Momma's hands, Momma's finger, seeing how she breathed. Momma stopped turning, and the *rhun-rhun-rhun* of the car stopped, and this time the woods made little noises. "I think it's flooded," Momma said.

"I don't think I can get it started."

It was the boy who did it, who summoned the dangers. He said, "What if a bear comes?"

"Don't," the girl said, astonished, shocked, that he would do such a thing.

He said, "What if a big old hoot owl comes and lands on the roof of the car?" He sounded happy.

"There aren't any bears in these woods," Momma said. "Don't be silly." The dog's panting filled up the car.

"Well," Momma said, "I guess we'll have to hike home. Roll up the windows." They rolled up the windows, and then it was dark outside. If a bear came it would push at the car with its big paws, and the car would rock. A bear could pick that car up in one hand and throw it. If a hoot owl landed on top of the car they'd be able to hear the feet and the wings. That would be scary, maybe the girl would cry from being that particular kind of scared, but she would know the hoot owl couldn't get in. "Let's go," Momma said.

They walked. The girl held her mother's hand; she walked with her mother, holding her mother's hand, and she listened to the sounds of the woods, listening to hear the bears and the hoot owls. As if listening for them without pause would protect her mother from them, as the boy's speaking of them had called them.

The boy and the dog walked in front of them at first. "We're the guides," the boy said. He still sounded happy, and the girl knew how this was, how he sounded happy at things that were very dangerous and ought not to be done. But Brownie was there, and she knew the dog would protect them, and for a long while, walking down Old Clayborne Trail, the mother walking in the rut and the girl walking up on the grassy spine, the boy and the dog in front of them as guides, the dog panting as if this were simply the backyard going on farther than usual, the girl listening to keep the dangers away, and she had a kind of active ease, that what they were doing was sufficient to keep them safe. Between the trees it was dark, but on the trail it was not as dark, as it had been darker outside the car when they were inside.

The dog barked.

"Rabbits!" the boy yelled.

Back behind the trees the bear pricked up his ears and turned slowly in their direction. The hoot owl, as big as the kitchen table, hesitated in its silent flight and wheeled, dropping through the leaves without touching a single one.

The girl, stiff with listening, her mother's hand in hers, her mother saying nothing to still the boy, the dog, nothing to stop the boy and the dog from running on ahead, chasing the bouncing white tails of rabbits out of sight along the Trail, as if the boy were not in danger out of sight, as if they were not nakedly alone on the Trail without the dog to protect them, Momma just walking, and so the girl had to do it, despite the listening bear, the listening owl: "Donald," she called, hoarse. "Donald! You come back here!"

He didn't come back.

She held her mother's hand, gave up her brother for lost, knowing he wouldn't stay on the Trail, would follow the rabbits dodging off among the trees. She listened then for the bear, for the owl, and for the faithful dog and her lost brother, holding her mother's hand. She brought them around a bend, and Donald and Brownie sat panting on the grass middle of the Trail. She was glad, of course, and angry. "You don't go running off like that again," she said.

Donald patted the dog. "There must have been twenty rabbits—did you see them?"

"Yes," Momma said.

"I bet there's a thousand rabbits out here. Me and Brownie are going to come out here hunting," Donald said, and now he walked with them again but would not hush, explaining about the bow and arrow he would make, the rabbit stews they would cook, and it was very hard for the girl to listen past him to the woods.

Then he fell down, looking back at Momma to tell about how foxes hunted rabbits, and so he didn't see the stone in the way, and he stumbled and fell down, and so after that the girl had to listen for the bear and the owl and the foxes, and watch where her mother's feet were going so she wouldn't stumble and fall down and hurt herself or the baby in the belly. She was more than solemn now, more than silent, carrying them all through the woods, between the trees, down the middle of the dark with her listening and watching, her mother's hand in hers, her will alone keeping Donald from racing off again, her will alone driving away the rabbits that would tempt Brownie to bark, goad the boy to run off and go crashing through the bushes off into the dark forest this time. She watched for the places the rocks rose out of the dirt, the places where the wheel track was crossed by deep-worn cracks.

"Shall we sing something?" Momma said.

The girl didn't answer, horrified at the madness, the blatant irresponsibility of it, their thin little voices threading out into the dark, between the leaves of the trees, calling to the shuffling bear. So when Brownie barked again she was almost relieved, and called only once, "Donald, you stop that!" and let him go, some would be lost but she would get Momma home, Donald and Brownie proving themselves more danger than help just now, let them go, let the silence come so she could listen more strongly, keep her will spread in a magic circle that grew outward from where she held her mother's hand safe in her own. Let them go, she thought into the dark trees.

Maybe the woods weren't deep. Maybe the long far walk, made and taken, was two miles. Donald and Brownie came back, and ran ahead, and came back, until the girl was no longer frantic, saving her strength for listening, and for willing the dangers off in other directions, and for subtle motions of her mother's hand that steered her around stones in the tire track.

MAYBE IT WAS only a couple of miles down that abandoned road in the dark, and maybe there were no bears in those woods, and maybe in 1952 bears would have been the greatest possible danger to a pregnant woman and two small children walking two miles through the woods on a summer night.

"ALMOST THERE," Momma said. "Can you see the lights? Over there?"

And then the trees fell back behind them and they were on the grass, and the grass was wet, the sky huge.

MAYBE IT IS not mysterious. Maybe it is very simple, as simple as "She has a round head. And hair," as simple as a song. The girl walked her mother toward the house, and the girl was weary. She had brought them all home safe. Donald and Brownie ran ahead again, whooping up the porch steps and into the house. The girl held her mother's hand more gently now, crossing the wet grass toward the lighted house, where Connie stood on the porch with a lantern in her hand.

Connie called out something. "Well, there you are!" probably, or, "We were about to send out the search party!" or something else, but not angrily, nothing startling in the words, and the tone full of humor.

Momma laughed and called something back across the wet grass.

She let go of the girl's hand, and went on more quickly toward the house.

The girl, who was only three, her hands still, in fact, baby plump, who believed in bears and foxes and hoot owls and the dangers of darkness. Who spent long times digging in the hard dirt near the back steps, and was often startled, alarmed by words. The girl, standing on the wet grass in the dark that was full of sounds now, maybe by now the pickup was pulling into the driveway again, the headlights crossing Momma who might have waved, silly, showing that they were home, all a false alarm. The girl astounded, watching herself left standing here with her hand still warm, knowing but unable quite to believe that no one knew what she had done.

Her mother reached the porch steps, laughing and talking, and then turned back and called across the yard, "Come on, honey—come on along." The grass was wet.

The girl thinking words as she crossed the wet yard, trying them in her mind, as if her mind were fingers and the words things that could be lifted and handled. Thinking, What if a bear comes.

Don't.

Would you like to go for a ride.

We'd better, they'll be.

Having so few words yet, lacking still Eden, and cast out, and wilderness.

Trying, Car.

Momma.

Children: the boy and the girl, and the baby inside Momma.

Like this: within the forest a trail, upon the trail a car, within the car a family, within the family a boy and a girl and a mother, within the mother a child, and the dark leaves grew all around, all around.

"You must be tuckered out," Momma said. "She walked the whole way," Momma said, "didn't you, honey?"

"Yes," the girl said.

And Both Shall Row

MARGARET AND MAY were sisters, who grew old. But when they were small girls they had sometimes played a game of piling their hands atop one another: May's hand, Margaret's hand, May's, Margaret's: May drew her hand from between the tabletop and Margaret's hand and put it on top of Margaret's hand on top of the pile, and then Margaret did the same. They played the game easily, endlessly, and their hands slid smooth and warm, out and up, the pile of hands ever increased, ever escaped, rhythmic and pleasant, hypnotic, an infinitely repeated magic trick, the pile unchanged and always changing, skin sliding above and below. Each knew her own hand from her sister's only when her palm met the tabletop, and then she withdrew it and joined it again to the warm back of her sister's hand. A simple game. And then they grew older, and had each her own home. And then they grew old, and they lived together again.

They lived quietly, after all each of them had done and had not done, in a small house in Clayborne near the vanished farm where they had been born and raised. May was the younger by three years, and had been the taller and more restless. Now that she was past seventy, that restlessness revealed itself only as impatience with everything on television and with the inconvenience of her aging body, and as a steady pleasure in walking outside in all weathers, and in the remnants of a quick temper, which now had become a silent sudden fury that would send her tight-lipped from a room for a time. She had once dreamed of travel but never had gone more than a hundred miles from home; now she checked travel books out of the library, and in cheerful moments said that she probably knew more about far-off places than she would have if she had been to them.

Margaret liked mystery novels, and every week when May went to the library she brought one home for her. Margaret was still shorter than May, but both had shrunk through the years so that the difference was less than it had been when they were young. Margaret was the more domestic of the two and did most of the household chores, leaving to May the bit of a garden, the walks to the store and library, the telephoning for repairmen. Margaret's pleasure was knitting; she indulged herself in it, she admitted. Some of what she made she sold through a shop in the next town to antiquers and passing tourists, earning enough money to pay for the things she gave away, tiny sweaters for every newborn whose parents or grandparents she knew even distantly, lap robes for the less fortunate older folks at the county farm, a shawl or sweater every birthday for her daughter, Coral, who lived in Texas, and something every Christmas for May.

They lived quietly now, mornings spent on chores and errands, afternoons on short naps and the arrival of the day's mail and newspaper; after supper May suffered the news on television, and evenings Margaret knitted and May read or did the newspaper crossword puzzle. They spoke, of course, Pass the salt please and Hasn't it gotten awfully cold, but they had been so much together and all their lives so close to home that they seldom had news to share, or reminiscence, except for the occasional sudden memory raised by a song on the radio or the Christmas card from someone nearly forgotten. Neither was a churchgoer; both were casually friendly with people in the village, though few of their old friends remained. If they watched each other for signs of failing health, now that they were both well past seventy, they watched without comment, and usually without conscious thought or a clear preference for being the first to die or the last.

But then May had a stroke, which changed everything, suddenly at first, and then slowly.

That Saturday, late in the afternoon while May was in the public library, snow began falling steadily. When she came out and discovered it, and it kept falling thick and slow about her as she walked the half mile home, she surprised herself thinking of death. She heard herself thinking, *Just don't let it be like this. This* was the snow: this steady silencing peacefulness that piled down and down as if it couldn't get enough of its own calm prettiness, so that first the light went a queer grayed dark and then sound was taken, too. And *it* was dying. Walking steadily through the feathered air toward home, May hoped that she would not die in her sleep, all unknown to herself. She wanted death to be like the wild storms that whipped the smugness out of the snow itself and came at the windows so fiercely that they flowered with frost, as if in desperate camouflage. She wanted to be there when she died, to know it was happening and was wild and important. Walking along she smiled, just a little: indulging in such a silly, romantic idea of passion, at her age. As if anyone really got the choice of how to die.

SHE HUNG HER coat in the kitchen so the snow would melt off onto the mud rug there, and she went through the living room and put the two library books on the stairs. The house smelled of baking beans. Margaret sat knitting a particularly brilliant afghan, blue with thin stripes of green.

"Is it still snowing?" Margaret asked.

"Yes," May said. "It looks like it could go on all night."

Over supper Margaret said, "Did they have that new mystery?"

"I left it on the stairs," May said.

"Thank you."

May did up the dishes, and laid her slight headache to the close warmth of the kitchen where the oven had been on much of the day. The evening weather report predicted dropping temperatures under a clear sky.

They sat for a while together in the living room, Margaret knitting and May with the newspaper. At nine Margaret said, "Good night," and May said, "Good night," and Margaret went up to bed with her new mystery, and May opened the book on the Faeroe Islands.

An hour later May woke from a doze in her chair to the sound of the snowplow going by, its chains clinking. She still had a little headache, probably, she thought, from sleeping that way, and she put on her coat to step out onto the porch; the air, she thought, would clear her head. As she opened the front door, she heard the slam of the Newharts' storm door across the road, and Mickey, their oldest, came out with the snow shovel. He swung it, and the broad blade caught the yellow of the porch light. The sky had cleared, and the air was sudden on May's face and legs, windless and deeply cold, and she felt her nose pinched by it even before she had pulled the door shut behind her. Mickey whistled as he worked, an old soft melody that May almost recognized. The snow arched like a slow fountain in front of him, and his shovel rang against the sidewalk as bright as a color. May's eyes watered, and she felt the deep chill gather in her back like heavy wings about to shudder.

"Hi, Mrs. White," Mickey called quietly. "I'll do yours first thing in the morning, okay?" He stood, hatless, his jacket open, and his warmth stood around him like steam around a barn animal in the dark.

"Thank you," she called back as quietly. "That would be kind. When do you leave for Mexico?" remembering that his Spanish class was going there soon.

"Another week—Monday," he said. "No snow there!"

"I envy you," she said, but for the moment she didn't really. "Have a wonderful time."

"Thanks—I'll try."

"Send me a postcard, if you have the time."

"Okay," he said. "I will."

He raised his hand to her and went back to shoveling, four more swoops, and turned and went back to his house with the shovel light on his shoulder. May went inside too, her feet numb and her head still achy, but she went to bed pleased, glad she'd seen Mickey out there. He was a pleasure; watching him grow from a little boy to—what?—seventeen now had been a pleasure. She had put in her will that he was to have five hundred dollars, and she wouldn't be surprised to find that Margaret had done something similar. She hummed a moment, that melody he'd been whistling, and found the last lines: *"Give me a boat that can carry two, and both shall row, my love and I."* A nice old song; she wondered where she knew it from.

Her last thought before sleep was that tomorrow would be Groundhog Day, February the second. Certainly, clear as it was now, there'd be sun, but no groundhog could dig through that foot of new snow, even if he was awake, which she'd doubt, as cold as it was. So there'd be shadows, but no groundhog to see them, so what did that mean? She was pleased that there was no solution, that the holiday could only go one way or not, not one way or another.

She woke from an odd and saddening dream, somehow involving the smell of lilacs, something cool and round she could still feel against the ball of her thumb, and a distant worry that had left her lonesome over a bowl of scentless blue flowers. Then sleep thinned, the dream details faded to a quizzical memory, and she acknowledged the coming day to be Sunday, the morning after the big snow, Groundhog Day. She opened her eyes to white sunlight across her east window, and remembered with a start that she'd forgotten to take that chicken out of the freezer as Margaret had asked her to. Wearily, she saw in her mind how Margaret's face would look when she told her, not angry but something softer—a kind of patient disappointment and willingness to pretend that it didn't really matter. An eagerness to pretend that, an eagerness to show herself, for the thousandth time, able to cope with May's mistake, able to work smoothly around it. May's irritation rose vivid and habitual, thinking this, and so, when her right arm jerked into the air before her very eyes, such a thing seemed impossible, or if possible only a manifestation of the irritation, but when her arm dropped and flailed up again she had time behind her astonishment to wish for the snug weight of her blankets to keep this wildness still. The sudden dark heaviness behind her eyes seemed, for the space of a blink in which she felt a morning grit in the outside corner of her eye, the desired restriction, before it became instead more like waking with the bedclothes wound over her face, and she was surrounded by a rushing wheeze that might in this pressing darkness be some large dangerous machine. Her right leg pumped, and she was grateful to its independence, because she couldn't do a thing herself to get free.

And then her body stopped and lay blind and motionless, askew but not uncomfortable, as she floated off, lighter than she had been in many years.

After a time, Margaret said, "May? May?" from some way off, and then May felt the cool shadow of her intruding upon the lightness of the floating, which had by now nearly become the gentle wrapping that could hold her whole self resting. She felt Margaret loom, huge, and felt herself gather to pull back, but her effort was as puny as a dreamed shriek. Helpless to escape it, she drew in with Margaret's mousy breath the cold salty sweat of an old woman's terror, drew it in heavy at the back of her mouth. She wondered sternly whose terror that was, in this silent room.

II.

FOR A LONG time May watched the large white surfaces, white but with areas brighter and less bright, flawless, nowhere quite shadowed. Two identical surfaces, identical in the areas of more and less brightness. But one was as if miniature, or distant, and both were present in the same watching. Watching them, seeing how they were identical but would not merge, made her head ache. When the aching had carried almost to nausea, a shadow came in front of her. Two shadows, one close, the other far off and made tiny by the distance. She noted, bored, that the shadow was someone, before she closed her eyes again.

MAY HUNCHED her shoulder, trying to slide the blanket back up over her arm without coming awake, but her arm was still outside the covers, chilled. The smell of potatoes came faintly to her, and quiet voices spoke at a distance. Television; she hoped Margaret was keeping an eye on the potatoes so they didn't boil away. For herself, she was tired, and meant to have this nap, since she'd begun it. She turned in the bed to get that cold left arm into the warmth and get back to sleep.

But did not turn, herself heavy, too heavy, the bed a magnet to herself iron.

Age, age, what a pain, as Mickey said, what a pain. So she reached with her right hand under the covers to move them up.

But the hand was not there, nothing moving under the covers, not even numbness.

Above her the white surface. She closed her eyes, breathing quickly. Under the cold fingers of her left hand something smooth and hard, the phone ringing, a radio announcer repeating, a woman laughing quietly but far off.

Margaret? she called.

"Grah."

She could feel how her arm was bound, immovable.

Margaret! she screamed.

"Nawh."

"Mrs. White?"

The smell of soap, a hand warm on her shoulder.

"Mrs. White, can you hear me? You're in the hospital," a woman's voice, not young, soft and clear. "You've had a stroke, Mrs. White, and you're in the hospital. You're all right. I'm your nurse, Jenny Morse, and I'm right here. Can you open your eyes?"

Graying black hair drawn back, eyeglasses.

"There, now—that's better, isn't it? You're in the intensive care unit, so you're not alone at all; we're right here very close all the time. You don't need to worry at all, we're taking very good care of you." The covers came back up where they belonged. "Now, you have an intravenous tube in your left arm, an IV—can you feel the tape here? We've taped the IV in so it won't slip out, and we've taped a little board under your arm to keep it stable. Do you understand, Mrs. White? Can you nod your head? Good. That's good. So that's the IV, and you can't do it any harm, so you don't have to be careful of it or anything. And you have a catheter—do you know what that is? It drains the urine from your bladder. So if you feel the need to urinate you just go right ahead, the tube will take care of it, you don't need to worry about that, either."

The hand again, warm on her forehead, smoothing her hair back.

"That's okay, Mrs. White. It's okay. You can cry if you want to—I know it's hard. Terrible way to wake up, isn't it? But you don't have to be scared or anything, because we're right here to take care of you."

A tissue touched to her temple, her cheek.

THE GLASSY smell of snow and cold wool trailed off Margaret standing there in her navy blue coat, holding her purse with both hands in front of her. In the silence, the small, almost regular *beep-beep-bip-beep* continued. Margaret drew in breath slowly, the reflected light on her glasses quivering in double the time of the tiny signal.

"The Newharts drove me in," she said.

Again, only that rushing near silence and the soft high reminding of some machine, until the nurse appeared and said, "Five minutes," pleasantly, and Margaret went away.

MARGARET AGAIN, but without her coat, that old brown stripe loose as it had been for years now over her bosom; *why doesn't she sit down somewhere,* May thought, because Margaret's hands clutching that purse made her feel cramped.

"Are you in pain?" Margaret said, something quick and surprised in her voice. "May?"

And then gone, but then the nurse and Margaret behind her.

"Now, what's this, Mrs. White?" soft and kind, her eyes quick past May and then back, a scolding and a worry in her voice for all the kindness.

What can I have done? feeling herself motionless, alive, not stopping. But then, too, the cooling heat of tears down from her eye to her ear. *Crying again.* Again that smell of soap and the dry, gentle hand of the nurse.

"Now, what's all this?"

MAY WOKE to the steady pale light, and had forgotten the earlier waking, woke to the smell of coffee and the oddness of the light. The doctor appeared, white jacket, eyes and necktie the same blue, his arms crossed loosely over his chest; she adjusted, guessed him not a dream but not reasonable either, not a tall man smiling kindly down at her in her bed.

"Good morning, Mrs. White," he said.

She waited, distantly surprised that she knew him to be a doctor.

"I'm Doctor Knapp, and I'm seeing Doctor Emmons's patients this weekend."

She knew Dr. Emmons, of course, Hebert Emmons's son; his first name was Richard, Robert—some such ordinary name.

"Mrs. White? I'd like you to try to answer a few questions for me, if you would. Do you know where you are?"

May was surprised to discover that she did know, knew quite simply. In the hospital, she said.

"Bode."

She heard the word spoken, the strange dull grate of the voice. Some other patient; she knew now that there were others, just past the white curtains that accounted for the steady paleness around her. She must have been interrupted or drowned out by that other one. In the hospital, she said again.

"Bode."

"You're in the hospital," the doctor said. "You've had a stroke, Mrs. White, but we think you're going to be fine. Your heart's strong, and we've got you on medication to reduce the swelling in the brain. Though you gave us all quite a scare yesterday, you know."

He had an easy smile, his two front teeth just barely overlapping, but he looked and looked at her, waiting. I don't really remember, she said.

"Bode."

"All right, Mrs. White, now I'm going to begin counting and I'd like you to pick up where I leave off. One, two, three, four, five, six—"

"Thebba, ade, nigh—"

"Good," he said. "Now let's try the alphabet. A, B, C, D, E, F—"

"Chee, ade, hi, chay—"

"Excellent," he said. "Excellent." He touched her fingers firmly. "You rest now, and I'll stop back in later."

But May had heard her voice, her own terrible flat crushed voice, and she raised her wrapped and restrained hand to stop his going. My teeth, she said. "Bode."

He spoke as if in answer to some other question. "You have a little aphasia, a little language loss, from the stroke. It's not unusual, and usually it's temporary, goes off by itself. As you get stronger, as the brain settles back down, words will begin to come back. It's a good sign that you can still do the automatic things, the counting and letters—not everybody can. It's nothing to worry about, though. We'll do some testing in a few days. What you've got to concentrate on now is resting and getting stronger, hm?"

And that deep, shattered voice rose and rose, "Bode. Bode." Until the nurse came where the doctor had been, and May tried to tell her too, tried to point with the hand that couldn't point because they had taped it to a board, My teeth—I can't talk right without my teeth.

DAYS DISAPPEARED, if days were passing. May thought they must be, when she thought. She was bathed; she was fed; they freed her good arm, offered her glasses, her teeth. Thank you, she said, and heard, "Boat," quite clearly now "boat." The nurses came and went, and Margaret, and the doctors. Again and again she slept, and woke in sadness.

They moved her to a room with walls and a window that showed the sky, and time returned. Light came after dark, the nurses were tired or fresh, meals came and had to be struggled with, the spoon pressed and raised, the mess she made, the terrifying thickness in her throat when she tried to swallow. They changed her sheets: "Hold on here just for a minute, Mrs. White, while I slide this out." "Can you pull yourself up just a little? Good." "Are you warm enough, now?" "We're going for a ride this morning," and the hospital grew corridors and elevators, a homely girl who asked her to arrange blocks on a table, to count, to say her middle name, to point to the blue ball, to say why she was there. "Boat," May said, always, and shook her head, tears springing up again.

She tried, and could not: could not raise her right arm, hand, fingers, leg; print a word, her name, any letter, with the pencil and paper a nurse brought, her marks and the nurse's marks alike less meaningful than Arabic; could not identify the pictures on the cards the homely girl brought, the lines and shapes and colors resisting transformation. Lying alone, hearing visitors beginning to hurry in as the last supper trays rattled off down the hall, she tried: Hello. Hello. She thought the word with all her attention, and tried, staring hard at the ceiling, hello, and heard the harsh, blunt "Boat." So when Margaret came in, May said nothing at all.

She did not get better. Her body did not get better, and without it she could make no use of her mind. She could point, and she could push things offered away—a spoon, a glass, a magazine—and she could scrabble a pill from its little paper cup and get it into her mouth and could swallow it, with effort. She understood what people said; even the voices from the television were perfectly sensible, though the shifting forms on the screen carried no likeness anymore to people or objects. She could see, the early doubled vision gone now, forgotten. But she couldn't read, or write, or speak except to complete the alphabet effortlessly or to say her one stupid word, and even that without inflection, always flat and harsh, she couldn't make it question or agree or even urge, except by being louder.

Once she had thought blindness would be the worst fate, but she hadn't known then how tricky fate could be. She hadn't known that she could be left vision and denied printed words and pictures, that she could be left her hearing and denied speech, left a voice worse than muteness, that she could be left movement and denied her able right hand, left to depend on the fumbling of her untrained left hand. Left, she thought, and knew that there had been a time when she'd have found the phrase funny, left with the left. She remembered her romantic idea of being witness, participant, in her own death, that that would be the best way to go out. But she had never even imagined this, that she could be halved. She had never thought of it, and so could not have guessed that the halving would be the unbearable thing. That lying on the firm, clean hospital bed she would cease to bear it, in fact, would notice her mind repeating meaningless phrases to itself, *regional highs, regional highs,* dropped by the television weather report hours ago; *Doctor McLean, Doctor McLean,* stuck there from the hospital's loudspeaker; *reasonable time for you, for you, reasonable time for you,* left singing by some visitor walking past the corridor. That she would lie and listen to her mind being mindless and find it comforting, more than any bodily comfort the nurses offered, or any comfort she ought to take from Margaret's visits. That she would this easily fail to care about the weather or the date or the flavor of her food, about how and whether Margaret made the eight-mile trip each day to sit quietly with her endless knitting in this room for an hour or two. That her only real pleasure would come this quickly to be the slow swoon into blackness that followed the sleeping pill they brought her now each evening.

MARGARET SAID, "They want you to go to a nursing home." She said it standing up, and then she sat down. She had her coat folded on her lap, and held her purse upright on top of it, as if she meant in a moment to lift the clasp and open the purse. "I don't know what I can do," Margaret said. It was afternoon, the quiet time before the evening nurses came on and the business of supper began. Margaret sighed, quick and hard, and carefully laid the purse on its side on the coat on her lap, and sat that way, with her hands lying side by side on the purse. "I don't think it's a good idea, myself." She smoothed her palms in short strokes out from the center of the purse. The loudspeaker in the hall called for Mrs. Hamilton to dial seven, dial seven please. "You'll do better at home." *Dial seven, dial seven.* "I'm going to talk to somebody," Margaret said. "There must be something I can do." *Dial seven, please.* Margaret opened the purse and took out her knitting, something fine and white on four thin needles, like a spider's web.

III.

A WEEK LATER Margaret took her home, Mr. Newhart driving the two of them through a needle-fine snow. Margaret took May home, and Mr. Newhart carried May inside. Her bed stood now in the middle of the living room, and the couch had been removed. While Margaret put her to bed there, in the midst of everything, May wept. She hadn't even known until then that she really had wanted to come home. She hadn't known until she saw the caution and pity in the face of Michael Newhart how deeply she wanted to be in her own room, upstairs, where her helplessness would be private and distant, where she could lie in silence until she stopped being. None of this was seemly, none of it should have been allowed to happen; only the mistaken and capable vigilance of the doctors and nurses had prevented her dying when she should have. Only they and Margaret had kept her from her natural and spacious death, when she had first floated off that morning in her own bed in the dimness of her own room. Where now Margaret was not going to let her be.

Margaret brought her some soup for her supper, and fed her because May wouldn't even reach for the spoon. When it was over and cleared away, Margaret came and sat in her usual chair and worked on the blue-and-green afghan, which crowded the room even more. She told May about Tina, who would come every morning but Sundays to bathe and exercise her and irrigate her catheter and change the bedding. "She's from Livingston, but she's cousin to the Spicers, somehow," Margaret said, and told May too about Mrs. Watson, the nurse who would come once a week to check on her. "This Tina is what they call a home health aide. You can't afford private nursing anymore." She said how kind the Newharts had been, arranging rides for her and having her to supper a few times and making sure the walk was cleared, and all the time she talked she was knitting, shifting the brilliant blue drape of knitting to one side and the other.

"Well," she said, finally, and put the needles through the ball of yarn, "it's time for your pill, and time I got some rest, too."

In the morning Tina did come, a tall woman, heavy and pale, who hardly spoke. She did all that Margaret had said she would, and took no notice of May's tears of embarrassment at being done that way in the living room with the curtains open for all the world to see, even if the world outside was empty at nine o'clock on a weekday morning.

Afterward Margaret came in and asked, "Would you mind if we had the radio on? I've put the television upstairs, but I got used to the radio while you were gone—just for company, you know, so it wouldn't be so quiet. The music is nice." May made a little wave of her hand, meaning what difference, please yourself. Margaret seemed uncertain. "I'll just put it on low. If it bothers you, ring your bell. Can you reach the bell?"

Every day from then on the radio played in the kitchen from the time Tina left until supper was over. Then Margaret would turn it off and come and sit with her knitting and talk, about odd items from the newspaper, about soup she meant to make, the weather, the price of groceries, the size of the fuel bill. Sometimes she had gotten a letter, and would tell what was in it, or some little anecdote, worn and familiar, from long ago it had reminded her of. At eight-thirty, she would put her knitting away and bring May her pill and fresh water, and go upstairs to bed.

THEN ONE DAY Mrs. Newhart brought over a bowl of forced narcissi for May; Margaret thanked her and put the flowers on the table by May's bed, on the far end, behind her bell and water and glasses and the box of tissues. The next afternoon, after May had suffered again the discomfort and indignity of the bedpan, and after Margaret had silently cleaned her and taken it away and had gone upstairs for her nap, May lay under the oppressive perfume of the pale flowers and knew that she was likely to live a long time. Years, maybe. Like this, lying here unable to escape even the passive offense of the burnt-wire smell of flowers that had as little to call life as she herself had, forced into an artificial bloom that was their death. But they would die, and she would not. Unless she could make herself die, will it or act it, and that above all was impossible, she would lie here for years. So she was crying again when Margaret came down, because she knew that nothing was in her power, not even suicide. Especially not that grandiose act, because she could not even get free of the heavy smell of a bowl of flowers.

That evening Margaret finished knitting the blue afghan, and the next evening she knotted on the fringe, and before she brought May her pill she held the afghan up for her to see. "There," she said. "All done. I think it's pretty, don't you?"

May closed her eyes. The blue was too strong, she had had it before her eyes for too many hours, that blue vibrating against the green, and the small dim cobweb over the kitchen doorway, and the small corner of a kitchen cabinet, and the smell of the flowers—she closed her eyes. It was all she could do; in a moment she heard Margaret moving about, the ripple of the plastic bag she put the afghan away in, the jingle of the naked needles in the empty knitting bag.

"I think it is," Margaret said, very quietly, and May knew she was offended. Even that she could not escape. "I'll get your pill," Margaret said, and May was startled by her voice, the odd disgusted way she said it.

Which must have been why, the next morning in the middle of the awkward business of having her sheets changed beneath her, May thought of the pills, and wondered for the first time if they were strong, how many of them she would need at a time to float off and never wake up. They had begun giving them to her in the hospital because she cried so at night. She had cried, and called out, "Boat," sometimes, too, and so they had begun giving her the pills to help her sleep. The pills dropped her into sleep, sleep into her.

By suppertime she had thought far enough to know that she must notice carefully whether Margaret actually watched her swallow the pill. Then she would know whether she had any chance of hiding it instead of taking it, and she would need a place to hide it. She hardly listened when Margaret told her that Tina had taken a job at the Livingston hospital, and starting tomorrow a woman named Frances would be coming instead. She hardly noticed, either, that she ate nearly all of her macaroni with hardly any mess, or that when Margaret came and sat in her chair she had no knitting.

"One Easter Gran made us dresses just alike," Margaret said.

She couldn't hide them in her bed, under her pillow, because they changed all the bedding every other day. She could reach the drawer of the night table, but Margaret opened that drawer several times a day, for the hairbrush or May's teeth or the lotion.

"Yellow chiffon with a satin lining, quite elegant, really, but she'd used the same pattern as our school dresses—those smocks that buttoned up the back—just without the pockets. And I thought they were awfully plain."

No drawer, no cupboard, no pocket even, to call her own, not even for a week. If a week would be enough, if seven pills could do the job.

"I probably didn't look too thrilled. I might even have said they didn't seem fancy, I don't remember. But when they were all hemmed and hanging in Gran's parlor, I remember sitting on the settee next to her and looking at them, and she got the scraps out of her basket—remember how she did up the scraps of anything, those little rolls of scraps, fastened with a straight pin? We found dozens of them after she died. But she got out the yellow satin scraps that day, and by bedtime she'd made little rosettes. About the size of a half-dollar, probably. So for Easter we had little wreaths of yellow roses sewn on around the necks and wrists."

If she could get hold of a used envelope, she might be able to slide it between the mattress and the box spring, farther in than the sheet went. She felt with her good hand to see if she could get her hand in there.

"They were probably the prettiest dresses we'd ever had. I thought they were. And Father said we'd be the sunshine at the sunrise service, though I don't remember going to the church, or even Easter at all, that year. Just how pleased I was with those clever little flowers, and the elegant feeling of the satin lining. And, of course, how angry Mother was with us for snipping the roses off, that next summer."

:*Broken weeds simmered rank in the heat, and May's breath dragged harsh in her throat as she dug. The dirt was heavy and damp; it packed under her fingernails, coated her fingertips so she could hardly feel the cloth of the flowers when she reached into her dress pocket to take them out, so she had to look and count to make sure she had them all.*

"I wonder whatever possessed us to do such a thing."

The memory had come fast and strong, unbidden, and May's anger, too, as violent and unplanned: You never! It was me, just me! "Boat."

"Oh—you're right, it is time," Margaret said, and went out to the kitchen for the pill and water.

Leaving May furious, her breath whistling, and when Margaret held out her palm with the pill on it May fumbled at it, furious, and dribbled water in her hurry to be blank again.

"Good night, then," Margaret said when she had dried May's chin and neck and hand, and she went up the stairs.

But before the blankness came on, before the slow settling, May remembered it all, deliberately, the close heat of their bedroom and the lurch in her stomach as she cut the clinging yellow cloth, the panic that sparkled along her bones when Mother came downstairs with the dress and held it up to show the hacked neck. *What is this?* May didn't remember just why she had done it, what small quarrel or revenge it was; she was five or six at the time. *What is this?* The dress held that way and May staring at it.

We borrowed them, Margaret said.

Borrowed?

For a crown, Margaret said.

And never, not that day as they lay side by side on their bed through the long afternoon, banished and waiting for Father to come in from haying and spank them, and not after, as they lay hungry and weary with crying after the spanking and smelled the supper they wouldn't have—never that day or after had Margaret even whispered, *Why did you cut off my roses.* As if they really had crouched together, ecstatic conspirators, to steal the roses for a crown. For some game they had never played.

MAY WOKE SULLEN. She pushed away the juice Margaret offered and lay feeling the stickiness of what she had spilled drying between her fingers. Frances came, even bigger than Tina and smelling of cut onions even before she got her coat off. She was late, May thought, and hurried, and May resented it bitterly; she was sure it was the day for the bed to be changed, but Frances finished the other things and left without calling Margaret in to help her, just put on her coat and took up her purse and called good-bye to Margaret, without ever a single word to May, as if she were a stick here in the bed, senseless as a stick. When Margaret turned the radio on, May fumbled for her bell and banged it in her temper on the tabletop, and Margaret came hurrying. "Boat," flipping her hand toward the kitchen, meaning, Shut that thing off, but Margaret brought her the bedpan instead, and patiently took it away again when May refused to pull herself over on her side so it could be put in place. The mail came early, and when Margaret brought it in, May watched, sullenly, to see what she did with the envelopes, to see how impossible it would be.

But there were none. A catalog and a small familiar newspaper May had lost the name of. Though she tried, she could not remember it, as ordinary a name as could be, one she'd known for years. She knew the paper was free, that it advertised farm implements and used cars, had no real articles; she knew, bitterly, that if she could speak, if she could try out a few words, the name would come to her.

She refused her lunch entirely, and Margaret took her temperature, holding the thermometer in her dead armpit. "You're not sick," she said calmly. "If you don't eat you can't get better."

But after Margaret went upstairs for her nap, May cried, just thinking how she couldn't remember the name of that newspaper, and how Frances acted like she was nothing more than a kitchen floor that needed mopping, and how she couldn't even get hold of an envelope and would lie here like this for years, until Margaret fell on one of her endless trips up and down the stairs and ended up bedridden too, or dead.

After supper Margaret came again and sat with her hands empty in her lap, Margaret who any day could fall, die even, have a stroke herself.

"They used to have those dances at the high school on Saturday nights in the summer, I remember," Margaret said, "and Mother didn't like us to go—she thought it wasn't modest for girls to go unaccompanied. But Father didn't mind, so a few times he got her to let us go. Oh, and weren't we fine, walking into town all dressed up, and worried that our waves were getting mussed by the breeze!"

If Margaret fell, Frances would come eventually, or Mrs. Newhart. And whatever it was that happened, whoever it was who came, they'd put May in a nursing home, with all the others who should be dead, all those others drooling and crying and barking their stupid noises. With one of Margaret's lap robes.

"And Father would come and walk us home at eleven, though the dance didn't end until midnight. I remember once when we went, and Miss Locke was there, the Latin teacher? With her fiancé, and I was so thrilled at her being engaged, and dancing right along with all of us young people."

Or more likely the county home. Who would pay for a nursing

home? Her monthly annuity was less than a week's charges for a nursing home, her Social Security another week's. Margaret had less than that, unless she sold the house. Which wasn't even hers any more, but her daughter's, Coral's. Coral, off in Texas, made plenty of money and spent it all on herself. She wasn't one to depend on for any kindness; she hadn't even been back for a visit in ten years, and had quarreled with Margaret then, about money. And had an old sore grudge against May. May would rather be in the county home than obliged to Coral for anything. At the county home they had six to a room, she'd read that somewhere. She didn't even know how Frances was being paid or whether Margaret had ever found and cashed that last annuity check she'd had in her purse.

"They played 'Am I Blue'—remember that song? 'Am I blue? You'd be too . . . if each plan—' " Margaret laughed, caught her breath. "Well, it didn't sound like that when the band played it!"

In her purse.

"So they played that, and Miss Locke and her fiancé danced. I remember thinking it wasn't a very good song for engaged people, not a good omen—and she never did marry, you know, Miss Locke. But that night I was all aflutter watching them, and hoping he'd ask me to dance."

Her purse. She could already feel it, the firm square of it beside her under the covers. They would let her have her purse. They would have to.

"Of course he didn't; why would he? But I danced—Campbell Todd was there, and Eddie Garner, all the boys."

They might think she was senile, but they would let her have the purse, keep it. "Boat."

Margaret stopped. "It isn't time yet," she said, a little reproachful. She smoothed her hands over her lap. "Well, it was a very nice dance, is all. That was the night Eddie Garner taught me the slow fox-trot. And somehow I broke the buckle on my shoe, so Camp Todd gave us a ride home early."

Again, memory, rapid and clear, came on May without warning.

:The headlights of the car came wavering behind her in the dark and she stepped off the pavement onto the gravel, sharp under her bare feet. But the car slowed, fear turned in her chest. "Oh, May! I didn't know what had become of you—we looked everywhere—I was so scared!" Margaret leaning out the car window, the car moving slowly as May kept walking, her shoes and stockings in her hand.

"I'm sure it was the last dance that year, and I'm not sure we went at all the next year, when Gran was so bad that first time."

You broke it yourself, on purpose! "Boat."

Margaret looked at her watch, sighed. But May could still hear how she had whimpered, after Camp had turned his car around and gone back and they were alone beside the road in the dark, her whimper and then the soft pop of the strap breaking.

May took her pill without thinking, without planning to enjoy this last one, and so the blankness came on before she was ready, still wondering why Margaret had broken her strap and then pretended to Father that that was why they hadn't waited for him to come for them. The truth—and Margaret had known it then—was that May had left because Margaret had sent Camp Todd to dance with her. She danced well, unsuspecting, enchanted that Camp, as old as Margaret, would notice her. *You're a good dancer, little sister,* he'd said, and that was how she had known, and the hot blush had come up, and she had gone out and kept going, and wouldn't have gotten into that car for anything in the world. And so Margaret had gotten out, and Camp had turned his car around and gone back to the dance, and even then May had wanted to run off and leave Margaret whimpering on the roadside as she deserved. Even after Margaret bent down and broke her strap, even after May had heard the soft pop of it breaking, and had understood that the broken shoe would be the explanation Margaret gave their father for leaving the dance early—even then, May would have left her there, if it hadn't been so dark, and so close to home already.

"YOU KNOW you can't go upstairs, May."

May shook her head no against the pillow, and tried a new gesture, a Come here with her hand, Come here ceiling. Margaret came closer, and May made Go away to her, pointed behind her to the stairs.

Margaret peered instead at May's face, as if she'd be able to read there the meaning of this hour's gesturing and Boat, boat, boat.

May huffed, impatient but not discouraged, not yet. Her purse lay upstairs on her dresser, in plain sight, unless Margaret herself had moved it. If she could just get Margaret to think about the things that were upstairs, she might guess right eventually. She pointed again at the stairs, the ceiling, come here. "Boat." Nothing she could do about that.

"I just have no idea, May." Margaret looked behind her and back to May, who waited. "I'm sorry, dear—I just don't understand." She shook her head, then patted her mouth, thinking, shook her head again. "I'll fix us some lunch."

May had watched that morning for a chance to point out Frances's purse or Margaret's, but both of them had been empty-handed all morning long.

"Is it my nap?" Margaret said, flushed, almost shy at the kitchen doorway. "You want me to rest down here?"

May covered her face with her clumsy hand and shook her head, No, heavens, no.

Margaret gave a little sigh. "Well, it was a *guess* at least," and went back into the kitchen. She had opened a window out there today, and May could almost taste the thaw, the peculiarly thin wetness of the snow melting fast.

After lunch Margaret said, "I'm going up for my nap now. Do you want the blanket over you again, before I go up?"

No, but please bring me my purse when you come down: May

thought it clearly, word by word. She shook her head no, pointed again up and bring it, and because Margaret still looked so puzzled, she rubbed her thumb against her fingers—money. But Margaret only smiled uncertainly, shook her head, shrugged.

"I don't know—maybe it will come to me."

Later May heard her moving up there, heard her go into May's room, and she sent the thought of the flat square black purse as hard and clear as she could. Margaret walked across the room; that would be to open the curtains, for the light. Partway back. She pulled out a drawer of May's dresser, and then after a minute closed it, opened another. Gran used to say if it was a bear it would've bit you. The drawer closed, and Margaret went out of May's room.

When she did come down, she carried nothing that May could see and turned and went straight to the kitchen.

At six o'clock she came back in with May's supper as usual but paid no attention to May's gestures. So May ate and tried to think of a new way to tell her what she wanted.

Margaret came and sat, as she had twice before, with her hands flat on her lap. But tonight her voice was flat, too, and hurried, as if she had planned out what to say.

"The morning you had your stroke, I stood outside your door and knocked. I thought something was wrong. But I had never gone into that room without your invitation. You know that. So I stood there and knocked. Until I believed you must be dead or dying. So I opened the door. You were lying—all crooked."

For a long blank moment she was quiet, and May thought of nothing, and then Margaret drew a breath and began again.

"Arthur was a good man."

And May remembered that Dutch's letter lay in her second drawer, on top of the photograph of his parents, the man and woman years dead before May met him, before he began coming by to visit Father when she and Margaret were still children. Margaret must have come upon that old letter and finally, fifty years later, realized that May had kept it. And now Margaret was angry, fifty years late, jealous over a scrap of paper, now that Dutch and Father were both long dead. Over a letter she had saved not for anything it said (though she knew it by heart, from *Dear Nicholas* to *Your friend, Arthur White*) but because she had never had any other written word of his, of Dutch's. A thing Margaret may have understood, now: that May had kept it even though by the time she and Margaret had found it, Margaret and Dutch were engaged.

Margaret was still talking, in that flat voice. "When Mother was sick, that long summer, Camp Todd came around almost every night after he closed up the store. Then the next spring Will Hotchkiss wanted me to run off with him to New York. What would I have done in New York?"

But May was seeing the photograph that lay upstairs under the letter, seeing Dutch's father, a man as lean and tall as Dutch himself, and with the same mild sorrow across his brow, standing simply on the step of the porch, and behind him Dutch's mother, her hair somehow a brightness, as if the sun were low and shooting miraculously through from the side to find only that piled hair. Both of them looked straight into the camera, held by their son, the first of his pictures (he'd told her this, quietly, the first morning they woke together, the week his divorce from Margaret was final) he ever believed was true. Because of the light, and the eyes, and the thing that barely showed, the woman's fingertips a row of bright ovals resting on the man's shoulder.

"He was Father's friend. At first, for a long time, that was what I felt. When he came walking up the road that day, two weeks or more after Father's funeral, that was what I said. I said, 'Oh, May, we never wrote to Arthur White about Father and here he comes now.'"

:His hair and shoulders touched by the reddened light of the sun through the turned maples. His hat already in his hand, so he knew already about Father.

That same light, that same mysterious luster within shadow.

"Well. Those were strange years. Gran passing right after Mother, and then when everything had settled down again, Father. I couldn't imagine . . . romance. It would have seemed frivolous. After all that. A little shameful."

May lay with her eyes closed and felt the tremor in her throat that came with knowing, at last, that the two lights were the same, not halos but like them, that the mother in the picture looked that way to her because the light had come upon Dutch that way, that day. Her throat went tight with rapid grief, but she opened her eyes to keep from feeling it, that she would never be able to tell him what she had discovered.

"Arthur didn't claim to be madly in love with me. I don't think he even claimed to be in love with me at all. He was thirty-seven. He wanted a home, a family. And he was a good man, Father's friend. That was not a bad—premise. For a marriage."

Margaret's hands groped quickly just above her lap, as if she were searching for her yarn and needles, and then, again, they were still.

"I saw how things were, you know. I saw."

May remembered how she had gone to tell Margaret, gone alone one evening, winter, and found her sister folding laundry in her dining room, listening to the radio. May kept her coat on and couldn't imagine how to begin. The radio was playing dance music; she could hear from overhead the small noises of Nick and Coral in their rooms. Margaret lifted a towel from the basket and folded it into long thirds on the table, smoothed it solidly.

I'm going to marry Dutch, May had said finally, her eyes following Margaret's heavy hands along the length of blue terry cloth. When the hands stopped she said, *Next Saturday.* She didn't look at Margaret's face, so she never knew what she would have seen, but she heard, in a moment, the quiet sigh, and then, *Well. Are you sure you want to do that, May?*

Yes. Because she was sure, never surer of anything in her life.

The hands finished folding the towel into a compact square, half and half again.

Well, you're neither of you children. Arthur's forty-nine, May—that's a big gap, fifteen years.

May didn't answer. She would never call him Arthur.

Though you've never been flighty—I mean, it's not like you'd miss going dancing or something. Oh, Margaret said, and then she was in front of May and her arms were around her, the smell of the clean laundry, *oh, May, you know I want you to be happy, and I hope you will be.* The hug was brief but firm, and when Margaret stepped back and May saw her face, it was undismayed, unangry, unbetrayed, only a little concerned, a little polite, a little glad. *I do hope you'll be happy, May. Now—I imagine your ceremony will be very quiet? Did you want the children to come? And tell me what you need—why, I've been waiting years to give you a wedding present!*

And that night, alone, her rage at Margaret's lack of care, as if Dutch were nothing, had never been anything, to have or to lose.

Now, after all these years, now Margaret cared, the flatness of her voice buckling into self-righteousness, into blame. "And I let it happen. Not that I could have stopped it—your—well. Your being drawn to him. Him being drawn to you. I knew about it before he did, long before you did, May. And there were things I could have done to keep him. Just for the children, May, I could have. Just because of the embarrassment.

"But the way I saw it was that he loved Father, really. I think he was glad about our first baby just for the chance to name him after Father. So why wouldn't he be attracted to you, too, and what real difference did that make? Oh, for a while I thought he'd get it out of his system, somehow, and then we'd just go on. The house and the children." She gave a bitter little laugh. "I even worried for a while that you didn't care for him. That way. But then I saw you did; I saw it before you knew it, even. I wasn't blind, you know—I did know my husband.

"And even when I filed for the divorce, it was all right. I had the children, and they weren't going to lose him. Neither was I, really. I didn't ever—begrudge him. To you."

Because you never loved him. "Boat."

But Margaret was already on her way to the kitchen. It was past nine. She came back in with the pill and the water and stopped at the foot of the bed.

"I never snooped in your things, May. I was trying to imagine what it was you were asking for, and I thought maybe it was a sweater, maybe if I took a look in your room I'd see it, whatever it was. I wasn't hunting for anything. I wasn't snooping.

"I don't know why you'd do such a thing, May. That picture—you told me you'd burned all the pictures he took. And I never said a word, not a word. I respected your right as his wife."

May refused, shut her eyes again.

"If you had wanted to save one, May, I could understand that, a keepsake. He took some beautiful pictures of you. But to burn those, to burn the pictures of Father with the team and the ones he took of Mother—to burn all the ones that *meant* something—that picture of Gran in the peony bed? And then to keep that—a picture of people we don't even know, complete strangers. *He* never cared who the people were—*he* was worried about composition, about lighting—why, he took pictures of his own children as if he'd never seen them before in his life! Oh, I know—he was the great artist, the Photographer. Well, I'm not. I'm an old woman who doesn't understand about any of that."

May kept her eyes closed until she heard Margaret come around the bed and put down the water glass. "Here's your pill," Margaret said, and the anger was gone out of her voice, the hardness too. What was left was nothing, just words. But May didn't open her eyes. "I'll put it right here, then. Don't knock it off," Margaret said, and went away, but stopped at the door.

"I don't have a single picture he took of the children after we were divorced. You burned those. Or any of the ones he took of me. I guess you must know about art; that one upstairs must be art. But he took a number of good pictures of me, whether you know it or not. Whether you burned them, too, or not."

In the light from the hall May could see the pill lying on the table, but she let it lie there. She tried to remember Dutch, her father's friend, her sister's husband, her own husband. Her lover. They were married for nine years, she and Dutch. She knew that fact, and knew the other facts, that when he died she had nearly a hundred photographs of herself he had made, containing all the things they had never said or needed to say, all the conversations that would not go simply into words. He was a humorous man, quiet, domestic, but they had understood each other. They had made love often and passionately, but she could remember nothing of it except that they had. But their lovemaking and the pictures had been enough for May's need of him, and she remembered that that need had been great. When he died, after six months of increasing pain and two long weeks of utter physical failure, she had gone home from the hospital and read the portraits of herself one last time. She remembered sitting at the kitchen table in their empty apartment over the studio, but she couldn't remember her own face in any of the pictures. And then before she had called Margaret to tell her that he was dead, she had burned all those pictures and all the other prints from his files, standing over the incinerator barrel out back in the hot late afternoon.

She had sold the studio and divided the money equally between his children, Coral, who still blamed her for the divorce, and Nick, who would never be responsible. Sold the studio and moved to the apartment behind the principal's house and went on. She was forty-four then. She had her job as a supervisor with the telephone company, work she did with care and well, though she was never popular with the other women. She was a widow, as if she had never been young, as if her life had begun when Dutch took that first picture and showed her herself beloved. Now that he was gone and the pictures were gone, she herself had become loss. That was why she had kept that one picture, which had been loss before her own, Dutch's own loss that he had made into a shape, with the light. And she had kept the letter because it was the first thing of his she had known to keep, long before she had imagined keeping or losing him.

But she could not remember now how the loss felt. She wished she could see that picture of his parents now. It had lain in her drawer for so many years, so many times she had opened and shut the drawer without even looking. She would look now, because she could not remember Dutch, any more than she could remember the name of that damned newspaper. So she took her pill, feeling for it cautiously in the dimness and in her clumsiness. She lay and waited for the blank heaviness of sleep, and she was nearly gone into it when she thought she heard Margaret on the stairs. But she couldn't rouse herself to be sure, and by morning she had forgotten even the thought.

She slept later than usual that next morning and was still drowsy when Margaret brought her her oatmeal. "It's hot," Margaret said, and hurried back to the kitchen.

She was wearing rouge and lipstick, and May wondered distantly if it was the day the doctor would come, poking and talking for five minutes. She ate, half listening to the rain and wind, a raw-sounding day outside after yesterday's balmy morning. She had nearly finished when Margaret hurried in and past, up the stairs. The telephone rang, and May could hear Margaret's voice but not her words as she talked for a few minutes on the upstairs extension. This must be Friday, which meant that the caller was Mrs. Newhart, who did her shopping, and now theirs too, on Fridays. May yawned.

When Margaret came down again she had on her hat, and May stared.

"I'm going into town with Mrs. Newhart," Margaret said. She picked up May's tray. "While Frances is here. You'll be all right." She took the tray out to the kitchen but came right back, so May knew she was leaving the dishes until later. "I'm taking that afghan to the store," she said. Her voice, flat still but a little high, admitted, as the undone dishes did, that an explanation was called for, that that was an unusual event. The lipstick was a bright line on her thin lips that disappeared as she spoke. She hadn't been to the shop herself since last summer, May knew for a fact. But Margaret didn't explain. She just went on past May to the closet for her coat and purse.

Margaret did it so simply, the swinging open of the door, the reach that May could imagine from the slight lift of her heel off the floor, and then the emergence, the purse strap over her forearm and the coat over that. She had the door shut and the purse on the chair and was giving the coat a little shake before May remembered, by surprise, and blurted, "Boat," too loud, too sudden.

Margaret startled. "What?" She stood for a moment and May saw how bright the rouge was on her fallen cheeks, how fallen, and more: saw Margaret's eyes looking at her, felt herself looked at and unseen. Or unknown, an anyone. And a jolt of outrage came up in her, of How dare you, and "Boat."

"I'm not going until Frances comes," Margaret said, to some whining child hardly worth the effort. She put her coat on and slipped the purse strap over her arm, the purse tapping her side as she did up her buttons. "You'll be fine."

May felt the least beat of fear and let it be fear that she wouldn't be able to make Margaret understand about the purse, that the moment would come when she put the coat and purse back in the closet for weeks again before May could make her understand. So: Come here, May gestured. Come here, and kept her jaw locked against her voice.

A car came up the road and Margaret turned away, pushed the curtain aside to see. "I don't know what's keeping her," she said.

May didn't care. There she stood with the purse dangling on her arm—if she would just come here where May could touch it, boat, point up, boat, come here, boat—she would have to understand. So when Margaret let the curtain fall back into place, May pulled herself further up on the pillows and put out her hand. Come here, Margaret. "Boat."

Again Margaret turned that face to May, and this time May knew where she'd seen it before, as if that face were all of their childhood, all the punishments she had gotten as Margaret stood by.

:Father thundering, the taste of lemonade in her throat, Mother in the kitchen crying, and May somehow to blame, that lurch of fear and confusion in her bowels, astonished even past defense, and Margaret by the door, that same neutral face, the same betrayal.

May roared, not even boat, just noise: she didn't think at all, and with her hand and arm outstretched she gave a sweeping push across the bedside table, sending water, glass, clock, lamp, flowers, tissues, denture cup, hairbrush crashing and flying.

In the abrupt silence the telephone rang. On the second ring Margaret touched her own chest lightly once and walked past the foot of the bed and into the kitchen to answer it.

May, breathing heavily, heard Margaret say hello, and I see, and no, I'm sure we can manage, and thank you, and good-bye, in a perfectly calm and normal voice, hang up the phone, dial, wait, and talk again. May lay and listened, but what she saw with her eyes closed hard was the pink glass water carafe Margaret thought was lost but would find one day far back on May's closet shelf, and Margaret's opal earrings she would never find stuffed down behind the couch cushions, and "Beloved Husband of May White" on the headstone, and then heard her mind saying, *You can't stop me,* and agreed, and thought, and grew quieter, and wished she had thrown something at the black purse that sat so smugly on the seat of what had been her own chair, not ten feet away.

Margaret brought the broom and dustpan and a rag back in with her, and put them down while she took off her coat and hung it back in the closet. May couldn't bear to watch the purse follow the coat.

She closed her eyes again and lay rigid, hearing the broken glass clinking as Margaret swept. *You can't stop me.*

"Mrs. White?" Mrs. Newhart in the kitchen.

"Come in!" Margaret called.

"Heavens—what's this?"

Margaret gave a little laugh, pleasant, amused even. "Oh, I was hurrying to get the phone and knocked against the corner of May's table and sent everything flying. Ah," as she straightened up.

"Here, let me help you."

"No, no—well, thank you. Oh, good—the bulb didn't break. But let me give you the list."

"I'm sorry you can't come—an outing would do you good."

"Well, I'll just wait for another time when Frances is here."

"Why was it she couldn't come today?"

"Mrs. Watson didn't say. But we'll be fine for one day. Are you sure you don't mind taking the afghan, too? Because it can wait."

Even after Mrs. Newhart had gone, and she heard Margaret drop the broken glass into the wastebasket in the kitchen and come back with the sponge mop, May kept her eyes closed, not thinking or remembering or doing anything except nearly trembling and keeping silent. Margaret finished, put the box of tissues back on the table, the hairbrush into the drawer, and brought a fresh glass of water from the kitchen. She crossed the room again, and back, and then the radio came on in the kitchen. Like any other day. Then May went ahead and cried, because if none of that mattered, maybe Margaret could stop her, because what more could she do? But she kept her crying quiet, at least, bitter, and had stopped well before Margaret brought her a bowl of barley soup for her lunch, without a word, without a washcloth, even, for her face and hands.

So May didn't eat. She didn't even pull herself up on the pillows, but just lay and waited, angry again even after the tears. She was waiting for Mrs. Newhart to come back, and when she heard her at the back door, May said, "Boat," loud and intentional, without apology.

"Hi," Mrs. Newhart called, and then to Margaret, who murmured something, "Oh, I'll just go in for a minute."

"Hello, Mrs. White," she said, and May could smell the rain and the car. "It's raw out there today, I tell you—a good day to be inside."

Come here, with her hand. Mrs. Newhart stepped closer. "Boat," her finger trembled on the cold surface of the brown leather.

"My purse?" Mrs. Newhart said. She looked behind her to where Margaret stood in the doorway. "Your sister already paid me," Mrs. Newhart said.

May shook her head and forced her voice to stay quiet, tapped again, very gently, on the purse. "Boat."

"Something in my purse?"

No. May stroked the purse. "Boat."

"I don't understand."

"She's been wanting something," Margaret said, apologetic, and May couldn't stop herself, glared past Mrs. Newhart at Margaret. Who looked right back, that same flat look. "Don't worry about it," she said.

Mrs. Newhart said, "Well, I'd better get back. Mickey's come home from his trip to Mexico with some kind of flu, and I'd better check on him—he's been running quite a fever. This weather!"

May lay and listened to Margaret putting the groceries away, and then Margaret went upstairs for her rest, and May listened to the driven rain. Father shouting: that had been about the play, she remembered now. Belle Amers had talked her into trying out for it, what, in third grade? And Margaret hadn't tried out, though she could have. So when May got the part of the maid, and Mrs. Carolan said those who had parts must stay after to get their scripts, said it right in front of the whole assembly on Friday, May had just assumed that Margaret would tell them why she was late. She had walked

home with Belle to tell Belle's mother, who had given them lemonade and raisin cookies as a celebration. Then she had walked home
and into Father's anger. What had Margaret said? Mother would
have asked her, of course, long before she went to the barn and got
Father. Who was getting ready to come and look for her. What had
Margaret said, or had she just shrugged, that neutral face already in
place? And why? Why do such a thing, deliberately get May into
trouble? Jealous, May thought now, of any attention May got, good
or bad. She took some comfort in settling it that way: Margaret had
always been jealous. And so she drowsed in the dim afternoon to the
sound of the rain.

She woke to Margaret standing beside her bed. With May's purse
held in both hands before her.

For an instant May half believed that if she reached for it Margaret would snatch it away.

But Margaret said, "Is this what you wanted?" and held it out
to her.

She reached and took it as if still dreaming, but in a moment, as
Margaret still stood there looking, May smiled stiffly, and nodded.
The clasp was old and nearly sprung and so opened easily with just
the one hand, and the purse gave out its old smell of money and face
powder and something sweet. She felt in the side pocket and found
the smooth annuity check, already signed because she had been
going to take it to the bank on Monday. She pulled it out now and
gave it to Margaret.

"Well," Margaret said. She turned the check over twice. "Well, I
certainly should have thought of that," she said, and her smile softened, May thought, just a little.

Supper was omelet, and May ate well, her purse beside her on
the bed.

Afterward Margaret went back upstairs and came down with a
shopping bag. "I meant to get some more yarn today," she said, "but
maybe I'll just see what I can do with all these leftovers." She settled

herself and felt around in the bag. "Lord knows I've got enough to make something of, even just squares for a patchwork afghan. Clear some of this out—I thought I'd try to get that Enders girl to come in again this year and help with the big cleaning. She was a good worker. This is pretty." She held up a ball of clear rose wool. "It's left from that set I made for the Towers baby." She pulled a pair of needles from the cloth roll where she kept them and began casting on, counting in a whisper.

May pulled herself awkwardly up on the pillows and began to unload her purse. Wallet and keys, half a roll of hard candies; she smelled them—lemon drops—and tried to get one out to have, but they were stuck together and her clumsy hand wouldn't do the job. An empty prescription bottle, but she couldn't read or remember what the pills had been for. She looked slyly at Margaret, who scowled over her work. Best to be rid of it, anyway, avoid suspicion. She put that on the table, and then the keys as well. A clean handkerchief, still folded and neat, a handful of tissues, her checkbook, a pen.

"I certainly hope this Frances isn't going to have many more difficulties getting here. Of course it is flu season, I understand that. But Tina was so regular." And then, "Now look at that—what was I thinking of, size seven needles with this yarn." She slid the narrow ruffle of pink off the needle and raveled out the yarn, wound it back onto the ball. "Mrs. Watson told me Tina's gotten a job at the hospital, did I tell you?" She chose a finer pair of needles and whispered again, casting on.

May put the checkbook on the table with the keys and the pill bottle. An old envelope with writing on the back, and this she studied for a while, curious, almost nostalgic that she herself had once made these pleasant lines, the blue loops and points like embroidery on the white paper.

"You remember the Spicers, that Tina was related to—they had the milk route when we were girls. I think it was the same Spicers."

And the sound of the needles, faint clicks, like a fly against a window.

Not likely, May thought. That family had all been small and dark, quick people, nimble. About the opposite of Tina, to tell the truth. "Boat," she said, meaning not the same family at all.

But Margaret gave a start, and then a half laugh as she looked up. "Are you finding what you wanted?"

May nodded, but didn't move again until Margaret nodded too and went back to her work. She put the old envelope with the tissues, to be thrown away, and felt inside again. A bundle of hairpins held with an elastic band, another pen, and a card.

"Fiddle," Margaret said, something wrong with her knitting, which she held up to the light for a moment, and then pulled off the needle again, sighed, winding the yarn.

The card was printed with a picture of Jesus as a shepherd within a circle of gold, and with printing, a single line above the picture and many lines on the other side. A funeral card; whose funeral had it been? She looked at the face of Jesus, far too girlish, and then, with more interest, at the stream that flowed past him and the soft green plush of the meadow. Odd landscape for Israel, she thought. Looks more like Switzerland. Or Oregon. She grinned.

"Twenty-seven?" Margaret said softly. "It doesn't really matter, I suppose. I'd just thought twenty-five." She glanced up at May and smiled, seeing May smiling, and said, more clearly, "Of course, it doesn't *have* to be any certain number." She shook her head. "But I'm wearing this poor yarn to a fuzz," and went back to work.

Which was the first time May thought to wonder if Margaret was all right, because she almost thought she might be going to cry. Over the knitting. She watched for a moment, but Margaret kept on, slowly, and so she went back to studying the card.

Well, last fall she and Margaret had been to a number of funerals. The postmaster had died suddenly, and that had been a big funeral, of course. Then there was Minnie Todd, older than Margaret; a smaller gathering but more of them people they knew. And somebody else, somebody's father—oh, yes, Ackerman, Bea Ackerman's father, Bea who'd been a friend of Margaret's daughter in high school, years ago. So they had gone, because Coral lived so far off, and Margaret had always approved of Bea, how she raised her children and then when they were gone and her father got so bad she took him into her own home to nurse him herself. So this was from one of those, and the printing on the back was always either the Lord's Prayer or the Twenty-third Psalm, and given the shepherd this was probably the psalm. Well, she knew it by heart and couldn't say or read it anyway, so that could be thrown out, too.

Then the purse was empty, and she was about to shake it upside down over the edge of the bed, to spill out the lint and little bits of paper, when Margaret said, "Oh, no," very quietly. May waited, but Margaret only put the needles and yarn very slowly into the bag, and sat a minute picking bits of pink from her lap. "Well," she said, "if I can't manage a simple scrap I must be too tired to knit."

Or coming down with something, May thought, remembering Mickey's flu, but she said nothing.

"I think I'll go on up a little early. I wish I had a new book," Margaret said, and again that almost plaintive strain in her voice. "I'll get your pill for you, and then I'll go on up."

After she was gone and the pill lay where the pile of discarded tissues had been, May did upend the purse: she didn't want fuzz stuck to her pills, and Margaret would sweep tomorrow anyway. The wallet and the handkerchief she decided to put back in, the wallet just for a reason to keep the purse, in case anyone got curious. And maybe she could tuck the handkerchief into that inside pocket, still folded, and then every night slide the pill in between the folds, so when she had enough she could just take the corners and pull out the little bundle of pills all at once. She tried it with the one pill, and it worked, even all thumbs as she was, and then she put the wallet in the bottom and tucked the handkerchief back in, and snapped it shut. Like spring cleaning, she thought, all the old trash disposed of, a fresh start. Waste not, want not; well. But I shall not want, also. She patted the purse at her side and almost wished she had kept the funeral card. It might have done for a notice that she meant to die. Actually, she was glad she couldn't leave a real note, even if it might save Margaret a little trouble. Not that anyone would suspect Margaret of anything. Except negligence, maybe; someone might think she could have become confused, and given May two pills instead of one, or that Margaret might have been careless, and left the pills where May could get into them, like a child into the aspirin. But if she could write, what message would she want to leave?

None, she decided, at least nothing more than I did this myself, without anyone's help. No one would understand if they hadn't been where she was, lying here day after day and knowing how hopeless it was. They probably wouldn't even wonder. They'd just assume she'd had another stroke. Funerals for suicides were always so awkward; when old Mr. Sealey had killed himself with the car exhaust, for instance. They'd put in the paper that he died peacefully at home. Well, maybe there was a kind of peace to it, at least more than she'd had the past few days, trying to figure out some way, and certainly more than she'd felt the week or two before that. But with Mr. Sealey everybody had known better, and that was hard for his boys, you could tell. No sense in putting Margaret through that. It would be undignified, too, especially for a woman, for herself. To be lying there and have folks know she'd committed suicide. Been a bad sport, or something like that. The kind of thing May, at seventy-six, ought not to have people thinking of her.

Though she wasn't as old as she looked or as old as seventy-six sounded, she knew that for sure. She shifted in the bed, pulled the purse close to her side. Right up until the stroke she'd sometimes had those dreams, where she was no age at all, only the desired one. All the nerve endings were still in working order, and the imagination, unconscious or not. She smiled there in the dim silence of her bed in the living room.

This was a little like having the electricity go out, or being snow-bound, this lying awake late all alone. Once she and Dutch had come home late and found they'd accidentally locked themselves out; she'd had this same feeling then, as if she might do nearly anything, since the thing she had expected to do next wasn't happening. She'd dropped heavily into sleep after that pill how many nights now? Since a week or more before she came home from the hospital; weeks, at least, if Mickey was already back from Mexico. His class had been going to be gone a month, she thought. And now she had the whole night ahead of her, and the purse that had so occupied her mind right here beside her, with the beginning of her escape safe inside.

In the newspapers and movies, people always took a great many pills, probably more than necessary. She did wish she knew how many she needed. How many more days of stinky Frances, and staring at the same room, and Margaret's ups and downs. This morning's scene—well, Margaret had always been jealous, and was jealous again over a picture. She seemed to have gotten over it. They'd never really quarreled; considering the whole business with Dutch, that was quite remarkable. A good thing, May thought, but cautiously. This morning—no, it hadn't been a quarrel. If she'd been able to just go out and walk in the air, she wouldn't have knocked things over that way. She might have done something *like* it—a few years ago, she remembered, she'd punched her pillow so hard a seam had broken, and she'd worked off the rest of her temper hauling the vacuum cleaner upstairs to clean up the feathers. Lost her temper. Well. She'd gotten Margaret's attention, anyway, and the purse.

The house was quiet, the rain had stopped, and May lay listening for cars. She and Dutch had used to lie in bed sometimes and watch how the passing cars made watery moving light across their wall. Suppose there was an afterlife. Some wavery place like that light looked.

Of course, she didn't actually believe that. Never had. The dead were gone, like the past. But suppose you could meet the others who had died?

She lay and thought about it for a while, choosing and discarding possibilities like a child preparing for the three wishes. She would want to see Father, of course, and Dutch. But what would those people know about what had happened since they died? Would they care? She was sure they were more contented, more at peace, for not knowing some things.

In the silence of well past midnight now, May heard how carefully Margaret came out of her bedroom and down the hall to the head of the stairs. How she slid her hand along the papered wall of the stairwell instead of holding the handrail. How long she stood there in the doorway breathing softly, as May lay still and made, she hoped, no sign of consciousness.

When Margaret turned and went back up, still without touching the rattly handrail, still so quietly, May quickly decided that she must have come down to check on some noise she thought she'd heard, and as the excitement of having succeeded in appearing asleep waned, she found herself in fact comfortably sleepy. She thought again of the possible reunions after death, the possible rules governing them, and slept.

IV.

SHE WAS awakened by Mrs. Watson's busy fussing voice in the kitchen.

"I don't know what it is—you just can't keep girls on the job anymore. One week! I mean, we train them free, and the understanding is they'll work through us. But off they go, without even a notice."

She came in and began getting out the bath things, still talking. May gathered that Frances wasn't coming back, and that that was why Mrs. Watson was banging things around herself today; though she always stopped in on Saturdays, it was usually just to check, and she often spent no more than two or three minutes with May, checking her catheter and taking her temperature and blood pressure, before she went out and talked quickly with Margaret in the kitchen.

"Okay, give me a hand here," she said to Margaret, and together they changed the bedding, which was when May noticed that her purse was gone.

"Boat!"

"You're okay," Mrs. Watson said. "We're about done—there. That's better, now, isn't it?"

"Boat," May said, reaching toward Margaret, who would understand.

"Oh," Margaret said, and looked uncertain, but Mrs. Watson looked keenly at May.

"She like this a lot?"

"Why—"

"Sometimes they get a little violent, you know—no offense," she said.

"Oh, I think she just wants something," Margaret said.

The vague tone, the willingness to let Mrs. Watson addle her—that was what panicked May. She lurched in the bed, pulled herself over so she could see the floor, see if the purse had fallen in the night.

The floor was bare.

But in the bathing and the bed making Margaret and Mrs. Watson had been all around the bed. Either of them could have struck it with her foot without even noticing, pushed it under the bed, thinking it was the bedpan. May jabbed at the mattress beside her and got Margaret's eye. "Boat."

"Something wrong with the bedding? A wrinkle?" Mrs. Watson turned the blankets back, pulled the sheet tighter. "You got to watch that kind of thing. Once bedsores get started they're with you forever it seems. There now. Happy?"

May pointed to the floor beside the bed, frantic. "Boat."

"Drop something? Or does she want to get out?"

"Oh, she doesn't try to get out of bed," Margaret said, shocked. "Never. I don't know just what it is she wants now, but we'll figure it out. We don't want to keep you. Why, yesterday she wanted me to bring her purse to her, and I finally—"

"Boat. Boat, boat, boat."

But the two of them had walked away, out to the kitchen. May made herself be still and wait. Mrs. Watson would leave, she told herself, and Margaret would come back. She heard the swish of the woman's coat and the jingle of keys under the ceaseless voice. "Sounds a little senile, you know? What's she going to be needing a purse for, after all—or anything in it? No harm in it, but that's how it is. You know, though, you'll have to think about other arrangements sooner or later, and I'm telling you, it's easier to get them a bed if they're still in the real world most of the time. It's a shame, but that's how it is. You think about it, okay? And the new girl—let's see—" May heard a quick scrabbling of papers. "Ruth, Ruth Nestor will be in on Monday. She's just finished training, so you may have to give her a little help the first few times. I'd come and get her started myself, but we had four people quit in the past week—four people! Well, we do our best, but there's a limit to everything. You think about nursing home care, okay? You're not so young yourself—no offense—but it's a strain. Lakeview's a nice place, they can have their own furniture—not the bed, of course, but some things, small things. One lady's got a rocking chair, one old guy brought his pipe stand—like that. It's high, but nice. Good regular care, too, and the doctor in twice a week."

Whoever would hire a woman with so little tact for this kind of work, May couldn't imagine; she felt like slapping her. Of course she wouldn't, really. She didn't know that she'd ever slapped anybody, at least not since the days when you slapped fellows who got fresh.

Margaret came in, and May heard behind her the quiet of Mrs.

Watson gone at last. Margaret looked odd, maybe tired. Of course, she hadn't slept well, coming downstairs that way last night. Heaven knows Mrs. Watson wore a person out at the best of times. Poor Margaret. So May tried a smile and then pointed gently toward the floor beside the bed.

Margaret went to that side and looked, but May had to urge her with boat and another pointing before she bent down and looked underneath.

"Oh, yes—there it is, way back," Margaret said. "Well—ah," as she stood up again, "I'll get it out with the broom."

That evening Margaret sat again with her bag of yarn leftovers. "I've decided to try crocheting instead," she said. "And all worsted weights. I think that fine yarn was the trouble."

All day she had seemed subdued, and May hoped the work would go well for her. Mrs. Watson was right, of course, though it wasn't exactly the most agreeable thing to say right out to somebody: Margaret was nearly eighty, and didn't need the burden of an invalid. Well, she wouldn't have it long now.

"You know, Gran taught me to crochet. Those doilies she used to do. I got pretty frustrated, I remember, working away with that tiny little hook, and the thread would be so dirty by the time I got anything to please her."

That was better; May thought she seemed better when she talked. But though May waited, Margaret was silent again, the hook jabbing and jerking along in the lamplight for several minutes before she went on. "I never cared for crochet. It's dull to do, and too bulky to be pretty. Unless it's too fine to be worth anything. Like those doilies. Useless." She kept on for a while more before she held up the work, a piece about eight inches square in off-white. After a moment she shook her head, and May saw again how very tired she looked. "Some things just aren't meant to be," she said. "Me and crochet is one of them. Maybe I can give all this away." She nudged the shopping bag with her toe. "Or throw it away—I don't care which. I can't use it up." She put the square, hook and all, into the bag and sat with her hands in her lap, idle again. May waited, but then Margaret just shook her head and pushed the bag out of the way with her foot and got up. "I just wish I had some new yarn," she said, as if such a wish could never be granted.

It won't be long, May thought. Margaret brought the pill and water, and May took her time arranging herself to take them, so that Margaret said, "I'll just leave this," which was what May had hoped she'd do. Then Margaret said good night and took her bag and went up to bed, and after a few moments, May slipped the pill into the handkerchief.

It won't be long, she thought again, and wondered how Margaret would take her dying. She'd done well about the stroke, which certainly had been more of a surprise than this could be. She'd grieve, of course, but she'd get on. Actually, this was a perfect situation, with Mrs. Newhart being friendly and so handy. May thought she'd try to take the pills on Friday night, this Friday or next at the latest, so that Margaret would have Mrs. Watson right there soon after she found her, and the Newharts would both be home. They'd do whatever they could, she knew, and she knew too that Margaret wouldn't mind as much about asking them on a Saturday as she would on a working day. By Friday she'd have eight pills; to be safe she should probably wait until the next week, if she could stand it.

Her head itched. She hoped this new girl would give her a shampoo. Tina had, and though it was a pretty awkward procedure, she'd felt much better with a clean head and clean hair. It would be something of an indignity to go and die with dirty hair. Did they shampoo dead people? She supposed they did, but it was a pretty grisly idea.

Margaret would use Knapp's Funeral Parlor, of course; they always had, and there was no reason to change. They'd have the service in that pleasant room on the left as you went in; there was a larger room past that, but that was for bigger people than she was. Calling hours would be Monday and Tuesday, and the funeral on

Wednesday morning; that wasn't ideal, but most of the people who would come weren't working people anyway, but as old nearly as she and Margaret. So Wednesday. Born on Monday, christened on Tuesday, married on Wednesday. She trusted that Margaret would choose a sensible casket, not one of those big brass things. Though those were usually for men, and that was odd, as if there were something more manly about metal than wood. Machines and furniture, she supposed; that might be how people made that kind of decision, without even realizing it. Mother, Gran, Father, Dutch—all her people buried here were in wood. Margaret might get a little frivolous, but she did hope she wouldn't go so far as one of those pillows of rosebuds; May thought she'd mentioned to her after Minnie's funeral how uncomfortable that looked, though she could understand the idea. That and the glasses; whyever bury somebody in eyeglasses? Well. She had her navy dress, the light wool with the white collar and cuffs, still in the bag from the cleaners up in her closet, and she hoped Margaret wouldn't spend good money on anything new. The navy blue was good quality and still fit pretty well, the last she knew.

Knapp's did sensible work, too; she didn't have to worry about them dolling her up like some places did. She could almost imagine herself lying there, her hands loosely clasped below her bosom, the linen cuffs crisp against the wool. Of course she'd never actually seen herself lying on her back with her eyes closed, but she could imagine the rest of it. Not the biggest turnout, but the Newharts, Miss Groff from the library, Nan Hubbard, who, like them, still got around on her own. Friends of Margaret's, probably—some of the people she'd knitted for, probably. Willet Andersen, if his son would bring him, he'd be there, though they hadn't been particular friends, even when they were young. But Willet liked funerals, she suspected—the amusement of the old. It should be good weather, easy walking; the rain yesterday should have taken off the rest of the snow, and by a week or so from now there'd be that healthy dirt smell that had always made her think *loam*. Though she still didn't know exactly what loam really was. Didn't want to, thank you; she'd have looked it up years ago if she had. She wanted it to mean what she thought it meant. Loam. For a few seconds she could nearly smell it, here in the closed living room in the eternal bed, could nearly smell it and feel how spacious and dry the sidewalks always were early in the spring, how hollow and wooden footsteps sounded on the clear concrete.

MARGARET WAS on the stairs before May heard her. This time Margaret didn't stop in the doorway but came two slow steps into the room before she stopped and stood in the silence of both of them breathing.

And this time May was not sleepy after Margaret had finally turned and gone back up the stairs, slow and quiet. May could hear Margaret's breath draw with more difficulty as she neared the top and could hear how she stopped in the hall for a moment to rest before she went back down the hall to her room. Except for that pause May would have thought her sister was sleepwalking, her steps had been so slow and steady, her whole performance so peculiar. Almost as if Margaret herself didn't quite know what she was doing.

So May was just falling asleep when she half thought she heard a motor and voices outside a good while later. But by midmorning, when Margaret woke her with breakfast and the sunshine lay in pale blocks about the room, even Margaret's trip down the stairs seemed less strange, probably just checking, not quite awake but worried by some noise or some such thing.

That evening Margaret came and sat without yarn, hook, or needles. May was certain it was Mrs. Watson's nattering that had upset Margaret so much that she couldn't knit or sleep. It was a shame for Margaret to be distressed over nothing. May was going to take care of the whole problem. In a week or a little more, Margaret would be free to come and go as she liked. And get the living room back in order, too; it looked just terrible, May knew it did, like overstuffed chairs or old washing machines on a front porch.

Several minutes passed in silence before Margaret spoke. "I don't know how that place of Mrs. Watson's stays in business," she said. "Lakeview." Then, so quietly that May suspected she wasn't meant to hear, so quietly that she felt a thrill as if she were eavesdropping, "That's where I'll end up." And it was many more minutes before Margaret roused herself to ask if May were too warm, to mention flatly what a nice day today had looked like, to go for the pill and water; she said good night without seeming to notice that May had the pill still in her hand, and took herself, in that odd slow careless-ness, up the stairs.

This night May waited, arranged herself so she could see the doorway and the foot of the stairs. She practiced breathing as if deeply asleep, and she checked on the time now and then. It was after one when Margaret came down. May slitted her eyes and dared see that Margaret was barefoot and without a robe, and then she closed her eyelids lightly. As a child feigning sleep the hardest had al-ways been not to scrinch her eyes tight shut. Margaret came the same two slow steps toward the bed, and May didn't dare another look; with the hall light on Margaret would see, and then she'd know May hadn't taken the pill.

Then Margaret turned and went back, and May watched openly: the aftervision of the pale shapeless nightgown with the thin heel below it glowed for a long time after Margaret had reached her room again and May had heard the distant sound of her getting back into bed. Her last thought before sleep was like the singsongs of her hos-pital days, *Not a word, not a word,* though now beneath the phrase she wondered whether she meant that Margaret had said nothing, standing there in the dark (and why would she, believing May asleep), or that it was a secret not to be spoken of. This time May had been afraid.

———

MORNING CAME, and sunshine again. Margaret seemed brisker, opened the living room window a little after breakfast, and moved surely about getting things ready for the new aide to bathe May. May reminded herself that she now had three pills safe in the handkerchief in the pocket of the purse, which she now kept on her bad side, wedged between her arm and her side. She'd keep hold of it, too, and they could think what they liked.

"Hear that robin?" Margaret said from the kitchen, and May did hear it, that delicious liquid bit of sound. Wonderful. Like a brook, like the brook on that funeral card.

She had seen the picture.

She had seen the face and it had been a face, the water had been water. Hadn't she? After all those cards the girl in the hospital had shown her, those cards she knew were pictures but had made no picture in her addled brain? For a long moment she could hardly breathe. She had seen the picture on that funeral card. She believed she had. And she looked quickly from wall to wall of the living room, though she knew there were no pictures, before she thought of the wallet in her purse, and that there must be something in it, even a dollar bill would do, even an old sugar packet or something, so she could be sure. Her good hand shook as she reached across to her dead side and pulled the purse over to where she could open it. The wallet was heavy, but it opened easily, and there were bills inside, three bills. And she saw the pictures on the one she pulled out, as sharp and true as anything she had ever seen: a man with thoughtful eyes and an almost feminine mouth, a knot of white cloth at his throat; on the reverse a large building with columns and a fence around it, two flags flying, a few people outside the fence, on the street a car like they'd had when she was a girl. She could feel herself smiling and she could hear the robin, and she felt for the next bill, greedily hoping it would be different. The purse slipped, slid off the edge of the bed, thumped onto the floor.

"Damn."

Damn? Her voice, certainly. She could have laughed aloud in the second before she remembered the hidden pills, the pills in the purse, and felt an old tension in her bones to hurry, to get them back and keep them hidden.

Which was just the moment when Margaret came back in and crossed to the window for the third time that morning. May made no motion to her, no boat request for the purse. She'd have to get it herself, somehow, and just now she believed she could.

"No sign of her," Margaret said, as if she'd suspected it all along.

May wondered, and then remembered: the new person, Ruth something. Late on the first day, a bad sign, but she couldn't care: just maybe she would get well—could it mean that? But of course she must first reach down and get that silly purse back up where it belonged. She waited until Margaret was gone again into the kitchen, and then she put the wallet and the lovely bill over under her bad arm. She worked herself as close to the edge on her good side as she dared and put her hand down without looking, because she didn't dare add the weight of her head to that side—a fine thing it would be just as she was beginning to get herself back if she took a fall out of bed and broke something. That would be the end of that. But the purse was right there, upright, and she'd been reaching so cautiously she didn't even knock it over. She didn't dare check the pills, even by feeling, with Margaret in and out; she could do that tonight. She put the wallet and bill back in and shut the purse, put it over where it belonged.

"May," Margaret said, and her voice was brisk with irritation. "There's no sign of that woman. Now maybe I didn't hear right, or maybe there's been some confusion about the time, but I'm tired of this Mrs. Watson and her Metropolin Company problems. We've got to have somebody we can count on, and I don't see why we shouldn't ask Mrs. Newhart." She stood in the kitchen doorway with her hands on her hips as she spoke, making better sense than she had in weeks. "Well, I've given it some thought, and I'm not ready to give up the ghost yet. Or you either. I'm going to just step across the road and see what she thinks. She may not be interested—I know with a husband and two children she's already got a lot to do—but I'd rather she had the money, and even if she doesn't want to do it herself, she may know somebody else nearby. I'll be right back."

May didn't know when she'd ever seen Margaret so determined. Or why it made her think so guiltily of the pills she had hidden at her side. What would Margaret say if she found them?

By then May would be better.

Or not.

And if she wasn't better, Margaret wouldn't find the pills, because they'd be inside May.

"Damn," she said to the empty room, though she hadn't meant to say a thing.

One thing at a time.

But she was seventy-six. She didn't have time for patience, some miraculous five-year comeback: just in time to die of something else.

"They weren't home," Margaret called from the kitchen, and came in. "I was surprised, this time of day on a Monday. But I'll just keep an eye out for them, and meanwhile I'll get your lunch."

Afterward May was glad she hadn't let Margaret know about her small improvements. Late in the afternoon, after no call from the mysterious Ruth or the harried Mrs. Watson (and Margaret had announced, vigorous, that she wasn't calling anybody), the Newhart car pulled in, and Margaret put on a sweater and hurried out. The window was still open a little, and May could hear the voices, Mr. Newhart's low murmur, Margaret's exclaimings, little Eileen calling something to her father. Then the telephone began ringing, and rang and rang, and when it stopped the house rang with the phone's impatience, insistence.

Margaret came in the back door and sat down out there in the kitchen for what seemed a long time. If May hadn't been so put out at the phone's noise, she would have thought that was odd, and she would have prepared herself for something bad. As it was, when Margaret came and stood beside her chair in the living room for a second May barely had time to wonder how she could stand, her face so gray, her whole body crushed looking, fallen in somehow, before she said, "It's Mickey. He has meningitis." And sat, heavier than her old body could possibly be of its own weight, in her chair. "They'd just come from the hospital for a minute to get a change of clothes for his mother. She won't leave him. It wasn't flu he got in Mexico. It was meningitis. That climate. They took him night before last by ambulance." She stroked her hand once over her mouth. "He may die." May remembered the motor and the voices in the night. She heard how wrong Margaret's voice was, how its threads were showing; confused, unable to think of Mickey who whistled in the bright dark, May thought how Margaret's voice had thin sharpnesses all along it, like package tape embedded with threads or wires. "He's been in intensive care, and there's no change. His father looks terrible. His poor mother."

May remembered the white ceilings, the beeping of monitors, but no more. Mickey's shovel catching the light, ringing in the cold. But she couldn't feel it, Mickey dying; she liked him, he pleased her, and it was impossible, of course, a strong young man like that, seventeen years old. But she couldn't feel it, the terrible thing Margaret looked, couldn't feel *oh, no, this cannot be, let this not be.* She felt instead something like the premonition of rage: at her pitiful pleasure at seeing a face on a ten-dollar bill, at how she couldn't even die without days of planning and hiding, but a young whistling boy could escape all before him. She hurried even in her silenced privacy to correct that: miss all before him.

And then she lay in astonishment at herself for having thought not that Mickey deserved to live out his life, but that she begrudged him, envied him the luck of leaving it so quickly. He'd had Mexico, and then would die. That she should be the one who had to do the work and endure the guilt of making her own death, when he, with his energy and strength, he would escape easily. While Margaret sat still in her chair the room grew dimmer; it was time for the lamp to be turned on, for supper to begin, but Margaret sat, and May saw how the cords on the backs of Margaret's hands were sharp ridges, the flesh drawn away; her neck, too, was shadowed deeply as she sat.

"You wouldn't understand, though," Margaret began. May felt again the creep, as of wings sprouting on her back, that she had felt twice now in the dark as she waited for Margaret to turn and go back upstairs. Felt in Margaret's quiet voice a threat. "You just can't, if you've never had a child. Never lost a child." May had no choice but to hear it, as Margaret told it, at last, after all these years.

"I didn't even see Nick that day, only his arm, bent and resting on the open window of his car. It was a Saturday afternoon. July the twelfth. They were going to a clambake at the lake, and I'd offered to keep the children overnight, but Nick had said no. I knew there'd be drinking, and I knew how he never let Jeanette drive that car, but Nick said no, they'd pick them up.

"So Jeanette brought the children, little Tiffany struggling up those steep stairs, while Jeanette carried Travis, and the bag of diapers and clothes and toys and formula. I'd heard the car out front and just took that one look to be sure it was them, and then I hurried out into the hall to help Jeanette. Nick sat out there in the car, doing nothing.

"He wasn't always like that. And I've always tried to remember how he was before—he loved his bath when he was little. In the summer, I remember, his head smelled—oh, when he was hot from playing, it smelled rich. Rich as dirt. When he started school, and Coral was so disappointed that she couldn't go, he used to draw a picture for her every morning while he ate his breakfast. Her school picture, she called it. And how he slept, winter and summer, uncovered, no matter how many times I went in and pulled the covers up over him, all curled up like an ear, his hand under his cheek just like pictures of children."

She stopped for a few long seconds, and then went on, her voice flat and accusing again.

"And when we'd gotten the children and all the things into the living room, Jeanette told me they needed the plumber again, that the bathroom sink was still stopped up. Of course, I was irritated. I'd moved out of the house so they could have it, and they hardly bothered to pay the rent even half the time, so I was paying on both the house and the apartment, and I thought it didn't seem like too much to ask for Nick to call the plumber himself. Since I'd end up paying for it anyway. But I said I'd call. How long could they get along without a bathroom sink, with two little children? And I asked her if everything else was all right, and she said, 'Yeah.' Never yes, just that 'yeah.' Then Nick blew the horn, and Jeanette jumped like he'd poked her in the side. 'Yeah,' she said, 'everything's fine. We probably won't be real late.' She went over where Tiffany stood with her thumb in her mouth and touched her on the cheek—Jeanette was a good mother, I don't care what she dressed like. She said, 'You be a good girl, honey—don't give your grandma a hard time, okay?' And Nick honked again, and raced the motor, and Jeanette left.

"By then I knew what 'real late' might mean, and I'd made a rule for myself that they'd be back around one, no matter what they said, and I wasn't allowed to worry until one-thirty. By midnight I'd given both the children baths and put them into their nightclothes, and they were asleep in on my bed, and I was watching television, knitting."

She drew a deep breath, but it was hardly a pause, hardly a preparation for the rest.

"When he knocked on the door it was so early, still, and I wasn't expecting anything, and so I thought for sure somebody had the wrong apartment. Even when I saw through the peephole that it was a state trooper. Even when I'd opened the door and he'd taken off his hat and said, 'Mrs. White?' I was still thinking he was looking for somebody else, some other apartment, when he told me what had happened. It was like I wasn't even listening, just waiting for him to stop so I could answer his question, tell him which floor he ought to be on.

"But I heard. I know I did, because I can see it all, still, like a silent movie. Jeanette driving the car up that narrow dark track from the lake, and Nick drunk, mad already, and the tire sliding off into the ditch, slowly because she didn't drive like he did, like he would have. If he'd been driving it would have been more of an accident, hit a tree, probably. And then the car there with its nose in the weeds in the ditch, and so dark you couldn't see what color it was. Nick probably cursing, probably yelling after her while she was walking back down the middle of the track toward the party that was still going on down by the lake, going for help to get the car out. Her bare arms and legs white in the darkness, easy for him to aim at, even with too much to drink. So when he aimed the gun and fired it he hit her in the thigh. Thank God. And she would have screamed, surprised more than anything, and so maybe she didn't hear the second shot. Maybe he didn't hear the scream. I know the trooper must have told me some of that, or I wouldn't be able to imagine it so clearly, but all I really remember is standing there and waiting, and seeing the mark across his forehead from his hatband, and trying to pay attention and not look at the hat to see if he'd been sweating, see if the band was dark. So I don't know what he said. I don't think he said your son is dead. Your son shot himself in the head, tried to kill his wife, and then committed suicide on the hood of his car. I don't think he said anything that blunt, I don't really remember. I remember that before he left you arrived, May. And then Reverend Barnes was there too, straight from the hospital, and I kept listening for the children to wake up. They didn't, but then Jeanette's father and brother came, and they must have been the ones who told me she'd be all right. I never saw her again, you know, so it was a comfort to know. And they took the children with them, both of them still sound asleep, and I remember standing in the hall waiting for one of them to come back up for the bag of clothes and toys, and trying to remember for sure if I'd gotten the extra formula from the refrigerator or not. I never saw those children again, either."

She stopped, and sighed, and May thought it might be over, or that her voice would change, would begin to have grief in it, sadness, anything soft. But it didn't, and when she spoke again her voice was hard and level, hard as stone.

"And then it was just you and me and the minister, May, and you said, 'I've got to get up early—I'd better go.' And you went. You never came up to me, never put your arm around me."

It was almost completely dark, darker than in the night, because the hall light wasn't even on, and silent, and May felt something like a swoon, a light-headedness that wasn't dizzy but just acquiescent, waiting for whatever would happen.

Nothing happened. Margaret sat still in her chair for a long time. They'd had no supper, and it was well past suppertime, nearly bed-time. Nearly pill time. May suddenly wished for the pill, wished greedily for its heavy covering of her mind.

"You never came over to me. Never put your arm around me."

And silence again.

"So I know," and now her voice was brittle, careful, "that you have no idea what it is like to lose a child. But I do. And I so hope that Mickey will not die." With neither hope nor sympathy in her voice, but she seemed to have finished.

She turned on the lamp, and then sat a moment in the light, and then went to the kitchen. She brought May a bowl of bread and warm milk, fresh water, and the pill for the night. "Just leave your bowl," she said. "I'll get it later."

May ate. Gran had used to give them bread-and-milk suppers. Graveyard stew, she'd called it. They had loved eating supper at her house, down across the road from home, Gran herself with her own bowl at the small square kitchen table with them. That had been a winter thing, as May remembered, and now it was spring, and the air here in this room was damp and warm, heavy. Maybe it would feel less close if it were dark, but Margaret had left the light on, and May lay still in the light.

The young trooper had come to May's door first. The same knock, the same certainty that there had been a mistake. The same "Mrs. White?" The same, "Your son has been in an accident." For a moment she had seen her son, who had been in an accident, and had heard her own voice from far off saying, "I'm sorry, but there's been a mistake—I have no children." Much closer, in the little hall where she stood, she had felt the young man who was her son, how he grinned in the darkness and how his shoulders moved just before he spoke to her, how his hair caught the light from behind him in the living room: not Nick, she had never much liked Nick, who'd been, she thought, a fussy child, too eager for attention, and then so sullen in his teens. Not Nick at all, but some son she had never known she had in her imagination. The trooper had stopped, of course, and somehow she had understood the error, and sent him to Margaret. "Wait," she had said after he'd turned away. He had stopped on the step and looked back. "Is he dead?"

The trooper had paused and then nodded, and gone on. She had stood for a long moment trying to see her own boy again, trying to hold the picture her mind had given her for long enough to see him, to see who he was, but he had faded as quickly as he had appeared, and all she had left, really, was the idea of his hair backlit that way. So she had driven across the small town, through streets empty even on a Saturday night, and the air had been a pleasure on her face and arms as she drove. Dutch had been dead less than a year, but she remembered no dread, no embarrassment as she went up the steep stairs to Margaret's apartment. No rushing sympathy, either, or fear, or wish to be of help. She went without choice and that was how she was those days, just doing what had to be done, without feeling any of it, since Dutch had died.

For a time, she lay as simply as she had driven that night, not wondering ahead of the arc of her headlights.

Who was it who had said to her, in some public place, some near stranger had said once, "Well, if you don't have them to laugh over, you won't have them to cry over." Who would have said that?

And why think of it now? Mickey wasn't a child of hers. She was fond of him, very fond of him, and she did hope he would get well. And why think of it back then, either? She'd never mourned not having children. It was just the way her life had turned out.

But when she had finally gone up those stairs and into Margaret's living room, it was true, what Margaret had said: she had not gone near her, had not said a word of comfort. Knowing, maybe, how useless such words or gestures would have been to her had anyone been near when Dutch died? Knowing, maybe, that she had been grateful to be alone those first hours without him? Maybe, even, wondering why she had come, and then the brother and father arriving, the whole confusion of the children being taken so quietly.

She hardly remembered what she had thought then, but here alone in the living room she had a rapid vision of Margaret that night: *Stark, her hair in pincurls flat against her head. As if she'd been barbered, shorn for sacrifice or penance, martyrdom. And her eyes coming at May, huge, engulfing, pulling her. Not a welcome, not a need, even, as I need you. Not I am in pain; comfort me. No. Something huge, something that strode past what May could do, anything she could do. Past and into her, as if she didn't exist, or didn't matter.*

May had stayed as long as she could hold herself free. She had not gone over to Margaret. She had not put her arm around her. No, she had not. She had not.

And Margaret had never spoken of it, rarely of Nick, never of his suicide, of the grandchildren, who would be nearly middle-aged themselves by now, older than their father had ever been. Margaret had never spoken of it all these years, and May had not thought of it in years, not since the funeral was over. And Margaret had never forgiven her. That voice tonight had not been angry, in all that telling: not even petulant or accusing, as it had been about the picture, about Dutch, which May had always believed was the unspoken charge between them, that May had stolen Dutch and Margaret had never gotten over the jealousy and embarrassment. But it wasn't Dutch after all. Margaret had never forgiven her, never would: that was what had been so cold in her voice tonight, that she would never forget what May had not done.

May lay looking at the shadow on the ceiling and felt that old resistance in her chest and neck, that old stiff denial: even in memory the voraciousness of Margaret's eyes that night frightened her enough to make her angry. May's own throat refused, the feeling that she could be swallowed down Margaret's darkness was so strong.

And now I will pay for it, May thought, as Margaret came down the stairs, not even careful of the noise this time. May lay fierce herself, her eyes open and defiant, not feigning sleep this time: *Come ahead.*

"I forgot and left the light on," Margaret said. May could see she had been asleep, and her voice was hushed and soft, as if there were some other sleeper she meant not to disturb. "I meant to come right back down—you can't very well sleep with that on," she said, and clicked the light off. "Good night," she said.

She was halfway back up the stairs when they both heard the car turn in across the road, and she stopped. One car door opened and closed quietly, and then the other opened, and in a moment it also shut. The night was so still May believed she could hear that the man's footsteps were heavy on his porch. But only one set of steps: Mrs. Newhart was still at the hospital. Mr. Newhart was probably carrying Eileen, asleep, or half asleep and savoring the comfort of being carried like a baby, though she must be nine by now. And he, too, savoring the comfort of comforting her this way, this night. Margaret waited until they'd both heard the house door shut before she went on back to her room.

Leaving May in the near dark. Perhaps if the sound from the Newhart porch had been different, or if she had not imagined for the man and his child that physical solace of bearing and being borne, she might have gone on with her memory of the night Nick died. Thinking how it was tragic, certainly, but hardly a surprise, the way Nick had been going since he was fifteen or so; how she was grateful at the time, and was still, that Dutch had been spared knowing what Nick had done. How Margaret had never been willing to set limits or to allow Dutch to, almost as if she wanted Nick to be wild, to prove that Dutch should have stayed with her.

But May had heard the footsteps of the tired and grieving Michael Newhart, whose son was named for him, and had imagined the warmth of his arms and chest as he held and carried his little girl, how strong she felt him to be, and that imagined comforting had comforted May, carried her past the memory of that night, past defensiveness. If she had gone to Margaret then, that night Nick died (and she knew this, without thinking of it or understanding how she knew or what it meant to know this), they could not have come to live together again in their old age, even as distantly as they had lived these past years. She forgave herself, and she forgave Margaret, because she had imagined that simple comforting in the dark, which brought her to thinking of how, so many many years ago now, she had sometimes sat on Father's lap with her face against his chest, and how it had smelled of him and of the barn, and how his voice had sounded when her ear was against his chest. How Mother's shoulder had been hard but comfortable when she'd held May to hug her good night or to comfort her after a tumble. How age had made Gran shorter than Mother and Father so May could smell her breath when she hugged her, and the breath had smelled of the cloves Gran chewed. And how she and Margaret had slept in the same bed, the warmth that grew where their backs touched under the covers spreading over her whole body, indistinguishable from sleep. And a game of hands they'd used to play, piling their hands atop one another on the table or the arm of the sofa; and then when May had gone to school she'd seen how the girls there played it, piling and pulling faster and faster until they were laughing and slapping. She and Margaret had never played it that way; it was a quieter thing for them, something they did idly, while waiting for visitors to leave or for Father to finish reading his paper.

She thought of Margaret this morning, confident and determined, and of the crumpled way her face had looked when she came in and said that Mickey was ill. She thought of her own morning's burst of hope for the return of some of what she had lost, the distant chance of reading and talking again, of something like a life. She thought of Mrs. Watson and her talk of nursing homes, and of the loss of Tina, who had seemed so steady. She thought, finally, of how she had thought that day in the snow that she wished not to die in her sleep.

So now she thought about suicide, the courage and cowardice of it. She considered the difference between a suicide like the one she had planned and the one Nick had committed. At first she thought that hers was a decision, his an impulse, but then, the night was so long, she wondered if he had not, perhaps, planned his, too. Maybe, at twenty and with a wife and two children already and no job, no father, maybe Nick too had found his life unbearable. Maybe that was how he came to have the gun in the first place, since it was a handgun, and he'd never had a gun before that anyone knew of. Maybe he had, in some confused way, arranged the night so he'd have the chance. And his act, which he might even have thought of as sacrificial, making it possible for Jeanette and the children to get along with their lives without all his troubles, his act had caused so much pain, even after all this time.

Hers would not, of course. In the first place, she had no intention of letting Margaret know what she had done. Second, she was an old woman who might have died months ago: Gran had finally died of a stroke, and she'd been five years younger than May was now. She and Margaret had grieved, of course, because they'd loved her, she'd been a part of their lives for so long; but there were no grandchildren, even, to grieve May. There was only Margaret.

Who didn't need the work and worry of caring for her. Surely that was true.

She listened carefully, but Margaret was silent upstairs. She took the pill and tucked it in with the others: four now. She listened again, but heard only a tentative bird outside and nothing from upstairs. *Surely that was true,* her mind chanted; *surely that was true.* She slept, and had a dream, and noticed even in the dream that she hadn't dreamed in a long time. She had a prism in her pocket, and was walking a dark wet street to meet her son, whose ship was docking somewhere nearby. She had a lot of time and had decided to buy a newspaper, because she would be able to read it now, now that she had the prism, wrapped in a handkerchief in her coat pocket.

V.

FOR TWO DAYS they waited, as if waiting were what they would do now forever. They waited for word of Mickey, listened for the car, for Mr. Newhart and Eileen, their voices, the times of day and night they left and returned. May waited, too, for some new sign from her body that it was returning to her, but it gave no sign, no sensation began in the dead half of her body, no new word escaped, no message appeared in her mind when she looked at the marks on the tissue box or the face of the clock. And she waited for Margaret to come and sit and talk again in the old ordinary way, or as she had talked of Nick, even; for her to turn again that chill disapproval on May from across the room as she had about the picture; or for her to come down the stairs in the dark again: for her to finish, somehow, what she had begun by talking of all those old things at last.

Margaret gave no more sign than the unreadable print. For two days and two nights the sisters slept late and ate at odd hours the canned soup Margaret heated. At the end of the first day Margaret emptied the catheter bag that hung from the side of May's bed, and as she replaced it she said, "I don't know how to do the rest." Not an apology, not even a worry, just saying. Earlier, when May had spilled some soup, Margaret had brought a wet washcloth and cleaned it up, but that was all, and May could smell her own body. The bedclothes were rumpled beneath her and skewed over her, but Margaret made no attempt at smoothing or straightening. She did no washing up in the kitchen, either, no sweeping or dusting. On the second day she got her coat and purse from the closet. "We're out of toilet paper," she said. "I have to go to the store." She went out, leaving May alone and waiting, not even apprehensive, just wondering if she would come back. The telephone rang and rang, again, but May hardly noticed, listening instead to Mr. Newhart starting the car and calling Eileen, his voice calm. "Come along," he called. Margaret came back, and put the bag on the stairs and her coat in the closet, and went on waiting, mostly near the front windows, as if they let onto Mickey's bedside and she were keeping vigil, as if she meant to hear something, some sound from the air.

That second evening, when Margaret brought the pill and then went back to the kitchen for the water, May heard her say out there, "I've got to get somebody." She came with the water and May looked at her, the odd grainy paleness of her face, as if she too were ill and unwashed, a pale grayishness, her face in the lamplight like a tissue from the box draped accidentally into the contours and shadows of a face. She put the water on the table and went again to the window, which showed only reflection this late. "Somebody has to go to town," she said. "I don't know who. We'll need food. Those pills are almost gone." After she had gone up to bed May counted and knew that this had been Wednesday; it was her sixth pill. Friday she would have eight, if they lasted. She knew too that Margaret had been wearing the brown striped dress since day before yesterday, had perhaps slept in it last night, was perhaps sleeping still in the same dress, and had not combed and rebraided her hair in that time either.

Without having to decide, May knew that she would not be able to take the pills if Mickey died. She knew it without having to recall the queer dim submissive air she and Margaret had moved through years ago when Mother was ill and then so quietly died, and a month later Gran had begun to die, not so quietly, raging and laughing and saying cruel things that meant nothing, until she too had been dead, and that second funeral, and then Father. Margaret and May had been able, so simply, to expect that death—anyone's, their own—was likely anytime. An odd period in their lives, and both of them so young, twenty and twenty-three when Father died, two solid years of death. She didn't have to remember that to know that they were breathing that same air now, already, that both had had lungs full of it when Dutch died, when Nick died. She didn't have to consider any of it to know that she would not cause Margaret to live out her days in that air alone, didn't even have to imagine how Margaret would be if she died, how the lassitude she saw upon her now would increase or change. Any more than she would have had to imagine the smashed and bloodied body of a dog on the roadside to avoid hitting the living dog as it trotted in front of her car. She didn't even have to decide that Margaret wouldn't be able to bear it, or that Margaret didn't deserve it, or that Margaret loved her, or she Margaret.

But she knew. She began to decide what could be decided. If Mickey lived, she might choose. If she got better, if they found someone to come in and help, if Margaret pulled out of this dull helplessness, she might just wait and see. But if she got no better, if Margaret declined, if no help came, if the decision were made to move May (even to Lakeview, she thought, with her own *things*), she could take the pills if she chose. She would know what she was doing and why, and she would choose the best for everyone. This was as close as she could come, she agreed, to being present at her own death; unless her body surprised her with something more dramatic, her death would be, for her, that last deep moment, that weighted dark comfort of the pills. The windows were gray now, and as she passed slowly into sleep she thought again of Mickey as he had been that night after the snow, how he had stood with the light from the porch behind him and talked for a minute. Her thought became a dream, and the plans had changed: the suitcase she held made her suspect that she, too, was going to Mexico. She felt shy about mentioning it, even when Mickey was in the car and called out to her, *You can ride with us. No, thank you,* she called back, careful not to wake Margaret, asleep in the house behind her, *you go on ahead.* Not minding the walk ahead of her, though she was anxious about how quickly she'd be able to go, whether she'd arrive in time or not.

The telephone woke her, the telephone or the sound of Margaret upstairs, hurrying from her room to answer the hall extension. May heard her stumble, or nearly stumble, or bump at least against the doorframe or table in her hurry to reach the telephone. Uncertain what she had heard, really, except Margaret's haste and the after-ring of the phone, May felt the lurch and hurry, felt the surprise of the bump herself as Margaret must, a step or two past the impact itself. Then she listened, strained to know. She believed, as she knew Margaret must, that it was news of Mickey, utter news one way or the other, or they wouldn't call at all. She strained to hear, but heard only that Margaret spoke and was silent, spoke again and was silent, spoke. Then a long silence, before she crossed the hall, and May heard the water drawing for a bath.

So it must have been someone else, probably whoever it was who had tried to call twice before when Margaret was outside, Mrs. Watson or one of her people, probably. So Margaret was having a bath, because someone would be coming, and though May could hardly be glad to have Mrs. Watson jabbering about, she would welcome a bath herself, a clean bed. Margaret was pulling herself together. They would get on a while more, May thought.

Margaret looked far better when she came down, her color was better, her hair neatly braided and pinned again, the brown dress replaced by a spring blue May hadn't seen since her stroke, quite a pretty floral print. She smiled at May as she went past, into the kitchen, a somewhat grave smile of course, but May was relieved to see it, and hoped that a bath would make her feel better, too, get rid of this queer fearfulness that she couldn't quite think away, this readiness for disaster.

Margaret brought her oatmeal with raisins for her breakfast, and though it was late, nearly eleven when she finished, May hoped again that someone was coming to bathe her this morning. It was another nice day, she saw, and wondered if Mr. Newhart had already gone back to the hospital; she'd heard him pull in last night around midnight but might have been asleep when he left if he'd gone back early.

"Well, we're going to have a try at a bath," Margaret said. "I'm not sure how thorough it'll be, but better than nothing." She got the basin and filled it with warm water in the kitchen and brought it back, and May thought she must have been wrong about the telephone call; maybe they had called to say they wouldn't be sending anyone today, and that had reminded Margaret that May needed care. Margaret washed May's face with plain water and then soaped the cloth, and as she stood soaping it she said, "Maybe I'll even take a try at changing the bed. We'll see." She washed May's hands and arms, and rinsed and dried them, which was when May knew that it wasn't going to be a real bath at all, that Margaret wasn't going to be able to overcome her modesty enough to undo May's nightgown and wash her really. May wanted a bath and a fresh gown, but the idea that Margaret was still squeamish, after weeks of tending the bedpan every day, tickled her. She half grinned and shook her head as Margaret rinsed out the cloth and got a grip on the basin to carry it back out and empty it. Margaret smiled back, just as May heard the car pull in across the road. And Margaret just smiled, lifting the basin. "That was certainly good news about Mickey, wasn't it," she said as she walked away, and then, over the sound of the water pouring into the sink, "I was so relieved—I can just imagine how his parents feel."

Which was how May understood that Mickey would get well: the call had been about him, and Margaret had not bothered to tell her until now, as if she might not have remembered to do it at all. So May didn't really feel relief about Mickey at all, but a quick anger, that Margaret would be so—whatever she was, selfish, thoughtless. Margaret came back in and opened both windows wide, hardly a glance toward May, but said, "Yes, that was certainly good news about Mickey," that same vaguely pleased way, almost as if she were talking to herself instead of telling May.

May's anger flipped in a beat to dread, the cold dread she'd been preparing for, it seemed now, the weight in her arms and chest: Margaret was not talking to her.

Had not been talking to her.

Maybe for days.

Maybe at all, since the stroke.

Some part of her was utterly calm while she rushed to deny: *but she speaks to me!*

As a woman speaks to a baby, or to herself in an empty house.

But the purse—she knew I wanted the purse, she knows I am here!

As a mother knows a baby wants a toy and pushes it closer.

But that about Nick—that was to me, to me!

No. To herself, to hear herself say it.

But the pills—she leaves the pills, she believes I know to take them.

But comes down later, to check. Yes, lying nearly asleep up there and wondering if she's turned off the stove, if she's locked the door, if May has taken her pill.

I have been less than the radio, May thought. Lying in the stale bed she believed it, that Margaret didn't believe she understood a thing she said, about Dutch or Nick or baths or weather or Mickey, any more than Mrs. Watson did, or the silent Frances or the silent Tina before her, or even good Mrs. Newhart, who had spoken to her, she saw now, exactly as if to someone's baby, with the same kind interest, the same kindness to the mother.

Unbearable: May was terrified, and heard herself nearly panting. What to do? Boat was worse than nothing, she knew that, and there were no gestures to prove understanding, to prove *I know what you are saying.* She could show Margaret the ten-dollar bill—point out the picture, *I see this.* But even as she scrabbled once with her good hand for the purse strap she could see how foolish it would be, opening the purse that way, and to no end. She couldn't prove anything, pointing to a car and saying boat, or even damn, if damn came instead. She felt a howl in her chest, the same feeling she'd had back in the hospital when she'd first heard her voice so crushed and harsh and tried to make the doctor understand.

She forced herself calm. *Today is Thursday; tonight is the seventh pill. Seven will do,* she thought. *And Mickey is getting well. That's all. It makes no difference,* she thought, *and maybe it's better, because if Margaret thinks I do not think or understand, she will not suspect at all, ever.* It did matter; she grew calmer, but sad, lost, as if Margaret had actually gone away and not come back. As if she herself had gone away and thought she had come back and had not, like a ghost who can't make people see her.

Margaret came just then and stood in the kitchen doorway. "It's funny," she said, drying her hands, and May watched her closely, trying to tell if it was true, if Margaret spoke meaning her to understand, or trusting that she did not. "It's funny, all these years. I felt better, after I went ahead and said it all out loud the other night. About Nick. I went right off to sleep as soon as I went to bed." She smiled, met May's eyes and smiled. May couldn't be sure either way.

Then the telephone rang and Margaret turned away, back into the kitchen and answered it.

Margaret must wonder, too, May thought. How could she be sure that May understood her, or even really heard her. Of course. Almost like calling into a dark room *Who's there?* knowing that there may or may not be an answer, and that without an answer there may or may not be anyone there. Or coming home, calling out *I'm home* into a house that seems empty. Or writing a letter. Or dialing a telephone even: believing or wondering whether no one is home if it goes unanswered.

So. She might try to make Margaret know that she was present and that she understood, and she might succeed. Nod more, gesture more. She felt weary just thinking of it, the struggle she had not been making. And, really, really: if she meant to take the pills—if she meant to die, why drag Margaret further into it that way? She would grieve less, wonder less whether she might have done more. She wouldn't have to worry about how May had taken the things she had said; and May, thinking that, felt a familiar little thrill of escape, as if she had something of Margaret's that Margaret didn't know she had.

"May?" Margaret's voice was soft, from the kitchen doorway, and May realized that her own eyes were closed. She did not open them, not yet. "Are you asleep?" Margaret's voice was soft but excited, as if she had a treat, a surprise for May, as if it were Christmas morning very early, or her birthday. Her voice was excited and soft, almost childish, the secrecy of it.

So May opened her eyes.

"I didn't wake you, did I?"

May rolled her head No on the pillow. But Margaret turned without seeing, turned to her chair and sat down.

"That was certainly a surprise to me, a complete surprise. Just out of the blue, without a word. Though she said she'd tried to call. Before she left."

She? She? And even though May did remember that there had been two separate times of the phone ringing and ringing, even though that fact stood in her memory as proof, May denied it, pushed away something that tried to take her breath away, something like panic but slower.

"I was sure I'd written her. Why in the world wouldn't I? Not that I'd want to worry her. Busy as she is."

Which confirmed it: Coral on the telephone, Margaret's daughter who lived in Texas, but was not in Texas now, had left Texas. Was somewhere much closer, and a danger. Margaret's face was calm, almost pleased, a little flushed, and her glance traveled slowly around and around the room, to the tops of the windows, the corners of the ceiling. But not to her hands, the fingers gently twining and turning around one another, lightly lacing and lifting free and stroking back, as if the fingers were bits of yarn she was working some new and gentle way. May watched only the moving hands, in her nose and mouth the earth smell of a cellar, almost the shudder in her chest at the sight of the long white eyes of the potatoes reaching out of the bin in the dark.

"I suppose I might have forgotten—just at first everything was very sudden, of course. Though, even years ago—years ago," and Margaret paused.

And May groped too, *years ago, years ago, years ago, Coral a little girl with red-gold hair, sturdy and funny, years ago she had been so funny when she was determined; years ago Margaret and May had been sisters counting their money to buy Mother toilet water for her birthday, back when stores let you smell from the bottle; years ago when Mother sent them down cellar for the potatoes and Margaret had always gone first.*

"Years ago we had night letters, remember? By the word, but so much cheaper than telegrams—we got that telegram from Aunt Jane when Gran was so bad, I remember. Such a funny message, too, where she'd counted the words. I don't remember exactly. And then she didn't get there in time after all, after all that hurry." She smiled, her face still vague, the eyes moving and moving, but not yet seeking, really, just seeing the four corners and the walls that joined them. "Oh, Father said to wire her. He said to, and gave me the money for it. But I was such a goose in those days!" She laughed, a small roundness in the voice, no more. "It never even occurred to me to get a night letter, which would have been the sensible thing to do. I just knew I couldn't send one of those awful telegrams that said something like 'Gran dying stop come at once.' I just couldn't do that to Aunt Jane. Of course I realized later that she must have been expecting it. But I just wrote a regular letter, a couple of pages probably, leading so so carefully up to mentioning that Gran really did seem to be fading fast. And then I rushed off to town and mailed it, so no wonder it was four days before her telegram came." May knew the confusion of it, that hurrying along the side of the road, how the sticktights grabbed at the skirt hem. Coral did not know how Margaret had been, was now. Did not care. Margaret laughed several soft sounds, and she shook her head, smiling at her silliness so long ago. "Five days before she arrived, and never said a word of blame. Now, Aunt Jane was a *saint,* May. Just a saint, never scolded or even mentioned that she hadn't been notified more quickly." She nodded and nodded then, almost rocking, her eyes going the edges of the floor, a little laugh, hardly more than a sound in her chest. "Well, well. Some things change and some don't, I'd say. Some don't."

May saw her catch sight of her own fingers and how they kept going gently round and between each other, saw her watch them for a long moment and then make them stop, saw her smile go flat and disappear as her hands went flat on her lap, palms down. "And Coral is no saint. Though I love her. She's my daughter. She has Gran's hair—when she was little, remember, I used to say that. And she always wanted things so badly. I remember when she was about eight, there was a dress she wanted, an apricot-colored dress." Margaret's face went softer, and May wished she could shout, say, "No, not now, don't think of all that now," but Margaret went on. "The funny thing is I remember the dress and I remember her talking about the dress but I don't remember if I ever got it for her. And she wanted it so much." Margaret touched the middle of her forehead with the fingertips of both hands. "Once, she was about twelve, I think, Dutch brought the children an atlas. The kind of thing he'd do, sometimes. Just bring something over, not for any occasion. He brought an atlas for them. And years later I was looking something up in it, and I saw that Coral had written inside the cover, 'To my beloved daughter, from her father.' That big round neat handwriting." She stopped for a long moment. "I wish I could remember about that dress, though."

May closed her eyes, remembering Dutch's handwriting, angular, light on the page. Coral had been an unpleasant child, she reminded herself, and Coral was no child now. She'd been no child for the past ten years when she hadn't found time to visit her mother.

"I don't know," Margaret said. "She used to be afraid of lightning and thunder, and Nick used to tease her about that. Tell her stories about windows exploding from the thunder, fireballs rolling across rooms. And she still wanted to follow him everywhere. And I remember her after Nick's funeral, how she managed things so well. She likes managing things. I do love her, but she is no saint." She stood so quickly May was startled. "Well, we have half an hour," she said, briskly, brushed her skirt with her hands, three quick flicks.

She looked about her, even put out her hand as if to catch hold of something useful, before she smiled again, such a bright smile, and sat as suddenly as if caught back by some invisible thong that held her to the chair. This time her laugh was sharp, and May wished she dared close her eyes and not see, because Margaret's face was so queer in the quiet after that laugh. But she didn't dare. And she didn't think, either, of what it was that Coral had come to do, because if she thought it she might make it true. Just as she knew Margaret hadn't said it for the same reason, and sat now with her face grinning like an animal's, the lips dry and thin and drawn back from her teeth.

:The cloth of the pillowcase so tight in her fingers it could tear,

already nearly the packed feeling of the dust that came from torn cloth under her nails, her arms trembled with gripping and pushing so hard.

May gasped, it was so vivid and surprising, the pillowcase so real to her fingertips. Which lay helpless and empty as usual beside her on the bed. Before she could think to remember when she'd ever held a pillow that way or why she thought of it, imagined it, so strongly now, Margaret laughed, and her fingers began again their stroking and twining. "It's so funny," she said, "the things you think of. Here's Coral, mad as a hen, driving right now from Livingston in her rented car, and I keep thinking about Lily Howard, that hired girl we had the summer after Mother's surgery. She came with us that summer when we went to the lake, remember? She was a great tall girl with curly red hair, and veins on the backs of her legs. I'd have been nine that year. I think we had plumbing at home by then, but when we went to the lake camp we had the outhouse, off a ways. One night just as it was getting dark, Lily went to the outhouse. I can still see her just as plain, how white her arms and legs were as she walked away.

"So I followed her. Mother was probably busy with the bedding, and I don't know where you and Father were, but I followed Lily, back a good distance and barefoot, and by the time I came over the little rise to where the outhouse was, she was already inside. I don't know why I went—maybe I meant to go to the bathroom myself before it got dark all the way, or maybe I meant to walk back with Lily. I admired her a lot; she was fourteen, I think, and I thought she was something.

"But when I got in sight of the outhouse, I began to sneak, and I went quiet as a mouse right up to the side of it." Margaret was smiling and frowning at once, her hands slower but tighter. "I heard Lily moving, and then I heard her turn the little wooden catch that kept the door shut, and I still didn't have an idea of what I was going to do. But I bent over, so my head would be about as high as her waist, and I stuck out my arms like this." Margaret leaned forward in the chair and stuck both arms out toward May, grinning tensely. "Then Lily swung the door open with no idea anybody was there, and I wiggled—"

Margaret began to laugh then.

"—I wiggled all my fingers and I said as scary—as scary as I could—'Oogely booogely boooooogely!'"

She laughed. She laughed and laughed, dropped her hands back into her lap, laughing.

She quieted herself, and tried to go on.

"Poor Lily—she dropped like a shot!"

Laughter swept her again. The only sound in the sunny room, Margaret laughing.

"She just—sank! Poor Lily!"

Margaret laughed and laughed. And May felt the cool packed dirt on the soles of her bare feet, felt the liquid laughing, felt herself collapse and sink beside the pale Lily, Lily laughing, the big girl and the little girl sitting there laughing, pained in their guts from the laughing, oogely boogely! There by the outhouse leaning, laughing, against Lily laughing, that starch smell of Lily, and tears had come and run helpless down their faces. As the tears now ran thin down her face, and she was sobbing. But it was Margaret who sobbed, searching blindly in her dress pocket for the tissues folded in a neat rectangle.

"Aahh," she said. "Ooohh my," and wiped the tears off. Shook her head at herself, ran the tissue beneath her nose, and grew quiet.

"Well. That was certainly silly." She looked at May and her eyes were dull, closed off, defensive. May's eyes were dry. She had not laughed, or cried. She had imagined, maybe. Guessed how it had been for Margaret. "I guess I'm just getting old. Forgetting the wrong things and remembering the wrong things." She rocked a minute. "I've always wondered why I did that. It was much more like something you'd do."

:The light from the hall fell short of the bed, and the pillow in her

hands felt too light, too thin. A blanket might be better? The door-
way scatter rug was dirty, matted under her bare feet; she should
have washed it, before.

Margaret patted her mouth, looking past May blankly. "But you
didn't, did you. I wonder why I did."

Though she stared at Margaret, May could hardly see her, a darkness crinkling at the edges of what she saw, thinking, *What is hap-*
pening to me, what is happening, the sensation of the unclean rug on
the soles of her bare feet and before her her own truncated shadow
in a silence. Which broke and fell away, rug shadow and silence, at
the sound of her own voice, "Damn," harsh, but shadow and rug and
feet gone so abruptly she slammed her good hand to the bed to keep
from toppling forward. Which was up, impossible, but Margaret had
stood again, her eyes on the front windows, and then May heard it
too, the car motor, and then the motor stopped, and the car door
opened and the car door slammed.

"Here she is," Margaret said.

SHE HAD AGED. May wouldn't have known her on the street.
Coral stood beside the bed looking sharp at her, and that was all
May could think of, how Coral had aged in the ten years since she'd
been home last. She was elegant, of course, hair shaped and makeup
smooth, her smell some combination of good clothing and good perfume and new car, and she had come in quickly, brisk and fit. But
May wouldn't have known her on the street.

For the first few minutes that fact seemed to May a protection,
as if Coral were truly the stranger she looked, with neither interest
nor power in this house, in their lives. She had heard her coming up
the back steps; Margaret had gone to the kitchen to let her in, and
May heard them:

"Hello, Mother."

"Hello, Coral—my, you look lovely."

And a kiss exchanged, and May thought, *See how she loves her,* but not in her own voice, in the voice of someone else, like a line from a movie she remembered.

"Have you had your lunch?" Margaret said.

"Yes, I did. Where is she?" The voice was unfamiliar, coated with an accent that was sharp and slow at the same time.

Then Coral came into the living room, and May saw her take it all in—the sickbed there in the middle of the room, the way May herself must look in the unmade bed with her uncombed hair, saw her take it all in without pausing, as if she'd expected something of the kind and the facts required only minor adjustments to match exactly. Margaret was behind her but came only as far as the doorway. Coral came right up to the bed, May thinking, *how she's aged, she looks like any prosperous businesswoman pushing sixty, I wouldn't know her on the street.*

"Hello, Aunt May."

May glanced past her, past the good gray suit she wore, to Margaret in the doorway, her hands going again but just the fingertips, the least little touches.

"Does she understand?" Coral said, asking Margaret without looking around.

"Understand?"

"Does she understand what people say to her?"

"Oh—why, I expect so," Margaret said, as if she had never really wondered one way or the other.

"Aunt May, it's Coral. I've come to see how you are. Do you know me?"

May nodded her head, felt how her hair pulled between the pillow and her scalp as she did.

"I'd have come sooner if I'd known," Coral said. "How are you feeling?"

May gave a little gesture with her good hand, a little "so-so" waggle in the air, and immediately wished she had made a different one—that okay sign Mickey sometimes made, or that thumbs-up one. She looked past Coral again, in apology to Margaret. Who wasn't watching, her eyes going the walls and corners again. *Shape up*, May thought, sharp as a nudge, and before she could stop it, "Boat" went out harsh and loud, and Coral startled.

That was when May knew her, in that quick little lurching hunch of the shoulders, in spite of the suit and the cropped and frosted hair and the oversize eyeglasses.

"What did she say?"

"Boat," Margaret said. "It's from the stroke," she said, a little resentful, impatient.

"Is that all she can say?"

"Oh, the doctor said it's not unusual. Nothing to worry about, the other words come back after a while. They call it something."

"Well, the doctor told me she hasn't made any progress at all, Mother, and I'd think it was something to worry about." Coral turned to Margaret now, and May could see her profile, how the flesh hung just behind her chin, how pinched her nose was below the big glasses. "How long since she's been out of bed?"

"Why, she doesn't *get* out of bed."

"She ought to. How long since she's been bathed?"

"We had a bath this morning, didn't we, May? She has her baths."

Coral turned back to May, looked her up and down sharp and quick. "What is *this*?" she said, and reached for May's purse, wedged between her dead arm and her dead side.

May slapped Coral's hand, hard, automatic, "Damn," slapped that ringed and manicured hand away from her purse. In the silent moment after, as Coral looked at her so, May put her good hand on top of the purse to guard it. She glared at Coral, who could do as she liked for all of May, she wasn't having that purse.

Coral nodded, and any slight resemblance to any child who'd ever amused May was gone as if it had never been. "You know you can't go on like this, Mother," she said.

"Oh," Margaret said, "now, we're fine. We've had these home health aides coming in every day—Doctor Emmons suggested the agency, and the insurance pays for most of it, they've been very good—"

"They've closed, Mother. You know that—they've been closed down, that's why Jim Emmons called me. Though I'd have thought he'd have done it sooner. You can't manage her, and you know it as well as I do."

Jim, of course—May had known it was some ordinary name, Hebert's son's name.

"Well, he doesn't know everything," Margaret said. "Right across the road we've got Mrs. Newhart, our neighbor and very capable, and she's agreed to come in every morning starting tomorrow. She'd have been here today, but her son's been sick—"

"You can't depend on some neighbor, Mother. Aunt May needs professional care. She needs to be gotten out of her bed, she needs therapy, she needs somebody overseeing her diet, and you and some neighbor can't manage that."

"She's a nurse," Margaret lied, but her voice was thin. "She's a registered nurse, and her husband—"

"No! And I don't want to be rude, but Aunt May isn't herself—she's violent, you saw—she may have Alzheimer's as well as the stroke. I can't be worrying all the time about you two, don't you see? Flying back here to see what else you haven't bothered to tell me? I have to know that you're being taken care of. I told you that ten years ago, that you were both getting frail, and what were your plans if one of you should fall, or get sick. Do you remember?"

"Of course I remember. I remember very well, thank you."

They stood a moment then, arms crossed, mouths tight.

"All right, then," Coral said. "I have made some arrangements."

Margaret waited, and May watched her waiting and kept her good hand firm on the purse beside her but thought, *Poor Margaret.*

"I have already talked to the doctor, and I want you to understand that he has approved of the arrangements I have made."

Margaret made a short nod.

"I have arranged"—and now Coral's voice was slow, almost cautious, and May thought, *She's pretending to care,* and nearly snorted, it was so obviously false, a trick, as if Margaret and May didn't know her, were clients, strangers—"for Aunt May to go to Lakeview Nursing Home in Livingston. It's a very good home, she'll have excellent care, and she can take some of her own things with her, if she likes. She'll be in a semiprivate room that has a nice big window; the other woman is a piano teacher, a very intelligent woman, who has also had a stroke. I've made all the arrangements, and you don't have to worry about the cost. What your insurance doesn't cover will be billed to me. I think the peace of mind will be well worth it, and the good care she'll be getting."

"And how am I supposed to get to Livingston to see her, if I may ask."

"Now, Mother—an ambulance will come for Aunt May tomorrow morning, and if you like I'll come and get you so you can help her get settled in. But I don't think it's a good idea for you to be here all by yourself, either—even with good neighbors, and of course you'll want to see Aunt May, as you say. I really think the best thing would be for you to move into Livingston, too. There's a very nice elderly housing facility there called Tower View, just a block from Lakeview, and you'll have an efficiency apartment all to yourself, with a little kitchenette, but with a nurse in the building, and emergency call buttons, and they serve a hot dinner every noon. You'll meet some new people, and I think you'll really enjoy it once you get settled in."

"I assume you've made those arrangements, too."

Coral nodded.

Margaret took a deep breath but kept her arms folded. "Well, then. And have you arranged for someone to come and help me clean and pack, or were you planning to do that yourself?"

"Why—" and May smiled, just at Margaret's sharpness: she'd taken Coral's measure, for sure. "Well, I wanted to talk to you first, naturally—maybe your neighbor would—"

"Her son is still not well. And she's a registered nurse, not a cleaning woman."

"You know I can't stay, Mother—my flight leaves late tomorrow afternoon, and I have appointments Saturday morning. It would be different if I'd had some warning, you know—some time to plan. But I'm sure there must be a cleaning service—I'll arrange it for—what day would be good? Monday?"

"Tomorrow would be fine. And I will need the dimensions of my efficiency apartment so I can decide what to take. I *can* take my own things? Well. If you'd be kind enough to get those for me, and hire a mover for Monday. You'd best get Willet Andersen's son, I think."

"All right. I really do think it's for the best, Mother. And you'll like it once you're settled—they have a nice bright lounge on each floor, and activities—"

"Yes. I'm sure it's lovely. If you could bring those measurements in the morning it would be a help. What time have you arranged the ambulance for?"

"Ten o'clock."

"That will be fine. I'll have May's things ready. And now, if you'll excuse me, it's getting late, and May and I always have a little nap in the afternoon." Margaret turned away and went up the stairs, steady and calm, leaving Coral standing. May felt tears in her eyes, *poor, poor Margaret,* who would have imagined she could be so haughty, and so quickly beaten. Beaten before Coral arrived, really. *Poor Margaret.* May closed her eyes on her tears so Coral wouldn't see them.

Coral stood a minute where she was, listening, as May did, to Margaret's steady progress to her room and the quiet shutting of the door behind her. Then Coral's indecision was almost a scent in the air, but May couldn't forgive her, not for any of it, not for making only one visit in ten years, not for coming now, not for how she'd kept herself away from Margaret even before she went to Texas. She couldn't forgive any of it just now, beginning to end, and the end was that Coral chose to believe May asleep, and left the house without a good-bye to her mother or her aunt, not even a touch intended not to waken. The very end, because May would not be riding in Coral's arranged ambulance tomorrow. She had the purse still under her hand, and seven would have to be enough. Coral would just have to cancel her Saturday appointments and bear Margaret's grief. Make some different arrangements.

The choice was clear, at the last. If anyone asked her she could say with complete honesty, I had no other choice. She reached a tissue for her eyes and smiled at herself. As if anyone would ask, as if she could say. Though who could tell? She'd never died before. Maybe someone did ask. In the quiet after Coral drove away, as May grew drowsy, she had the pleasant spacious feeling of being packed for a trip. She was nearly asleep when Margaret dropped something upstairs that clattered and bounced, so nearly asleep that the waking was a shock and she lay with her heart pounding.

Margaret came down the stairs. "I couldn't rest," she said. "There's so much to do. May." She came close to the bed and put her hand on May's good hand. "May, Coral isn't—May, we don't have to do as she says if we don't want to. Do you understand that?"

As she had talked once long long ago when Miss Benedict came to take care of them while Mother was sick, that same serious secrecy. May nodded; she knew that Coral's plans didn't concern her in the least, except for timing, but she didn't know just what Margaret meant, how Margaret intended to escape those plans.

"Good," Margaret said, but kept her eyes on May's for a long moment before she patted her hand and said again, "Good. Now. Do you want to go to that home?" her voice grown soft, almost a tremor in it.

And now May kept Margaret's eyes and felt that same tremor

down the center of her body, yielding and brave, telling the secret. And rolled her head gently no.

Margaret's smile shook too, and her voice. "That's all right, then. Now I don't want you to worry about it anymore. I won't let them take you." Her voice grew stronger, smoother. "Coral's just gotten a little bit big for her britches. Now," and she pulled herself up, released May's hand and eyes, "I've got to go to the store. Will you be all right? Do you need anything before I go?"

May hoped Margaret wasn't counting on Mrs. Newhart to get them out of this. Or anyone else, either. It was clear that Coral wasn't going to change her mind, no matter how many people Margaret might enlist. And she did hope Coral wouldn't call while Margaret was out. It seemed a big risk to take, leaving like that even for half an hour. If Coral did try to call and got no answer, she might change her arrangements—she could do that, May thought, get an ambulance here in an hour, before May could do a thing about it. May lay dry mouthed with anxiety the whole time Margaret was gone for fear the phone would ring. The danger of it kept her from wondering just what it was Margaret meant to do; she concentrated on the phone remaining silent.

Which it did, but when Margaret came hurrying in the back door she picked up the phone and dialed as soon as she had set down the bag, before she said as much as Hello, I'm home.

"Coral?" May heard her say. "Did you just try to call me? Oh. Well, I wonder who it was—I was up in the attic sorting through a box, and the phone rang and I came down, but they'd hung up. I just thought it might be you." A longish pause. "All right. Yes. Yes. Coral— Coral, I just want to say that I know you mean well." Another long pause. "Well. We'll see. Good-bye, dear."

Margaret hung up and let out a long breath. "Well," she said, and poked her head in to smile at May. "After I got in the store I thought what if Coral should call while I'm gone—it put wings on my feet, I tell you!" She laughed, a simple pure laugh, as she might have laughed five years ago, and disappeared back into the kitchen, but kept talking. "So I just thought I'd make sure we weren't in any more hot water. Wait till you see what I got for our supper, May."

She came in with something small in her hand, which she put on the stairs, and a smile, a satisfied, excited smile for May. "Eggs Benedict!" she said, as if it were a gay secret. "And they had fresh rhubarb, if you can believe that, and I'm going to stew some up for our dessert. I remember we had eggs Benedict and stewed rhubarb for supper on your graduation day, remember?"

May did remember, to her surprise, because she hadn't thought of graduation in probably forty years, but now it seemed to her, remembering them all in the old dining room, that that was the last time everything had been really all right, the last simple family celebration, Mother and Father and Gran all well and proud—she was touched and surprised that Margaret would remember that at all, much less the meal. May's high school graduation. She remembered it now, and when she smelled the bacon cooking the memory changed, as if it had somehow unfolded, opened, and had revealed at its center the present, these walls, this dusk gathering outside, this peculiar festivity in the air.

Margaret brought her her supper on the good china with one of the stiff old real linen napkins spread beneath it on the bed tray and another folded at the side, and then she brought her own supper in, on the same flowered china, and set herself a place on the table beside her chair, and the sisters ate together by lamplight as the windows darkened.

Then they had their rhubarb, still warm, in the footed glass bowls that had been Gran's, and then Margaret closed the windows and the curtains, and did the washing up, and came back to sit in her chair beside May, who lay, simply waiting, comforted and satisfied by the supper and gently sorry that Margaret would have to mourn her.

"I've been remembering, this afternoon, May," Margaret said quietly, and her hands were loose and still in her lap. "I was remembering one time when we were little girls and I got you in trouble about coming home late from school. I've always felt bad about that. I suppose I had my reasons at the time, but I can't remember what they were, now. I've always—"

The knock at the back door froze them both, eye to eye, guilty, the fear sudden up their bones, and May thought, Don't answer it. "Boat," she whispered. But Margaret rose quietly and walked slowly out through the kitchen.

:Single-edge. The box smaller than a pack of gum, the letters blocky and ornate.

"Oh, Howard," Margaret said. "Come in. It's Howard Andersen, May—Willet's boy. Come in."

"That's okay, I just stopped for a minute. I'm to come on Monday for your furniture?"

"That's right—Coral called you, then. Will Monday be convenient?"

"No trouble there, I just needed to know about how much stuff you're planning on so I know which truck."

"Which truck?"

"Yeah—the big one we could get your whole house in, but if you're leaving most of the big stuff, washer and dryer, stove, like that, we can probably get by with the small one."

"Oh, I'm sure we won't need more than the small one," Margaret said. "The small truck will do, I'm sure."

"Okay then, Mrs. White—sorry to see you leaving, though."

"Yes. I'm sorry to go, in a way."

"Bright and early Monday, then."

"Bright and early," Margaret said. "Good night, Howard—tell your father we send our best."

:She didn't draw with her fingertip on the steamed mirror, knowing how that left a film even after the steam dried off. Though she did wonder what she looked like, just now.

As Margaret came back in and took her place in the chair again,

May wondered for the last time what that was, that odd sudden something like a vivid memory, as sharp as a dream, that kept coming to her lately. Because Margaret smoothed her hands once, twice, on her lap and began again.

"I've been remembering. Lots of things you may remember, too— like your graduation day, and how proud we were of you being salutatorian. And that time we went berrying with Aunt Jane and Hal, and Gran thought she'd seen a bear. How you and I used to carry Gran's milk can to her from the barn, with the old broom handle between us and the can hanging from that, we pretended we were the Dutch twins."

Margaret went on, but May knew it all, sudden as a blow, the bits tumbling together like the end of a mystery story: she could read in her mind the chunky fancy lettering on the small package: GEM, it said: and that package was what Margaret had put on the stairs, she had risked Coral's calling to go to the store not for eggs Benedict and rhubarb but for razor blades, and the steam was on the bathroom mirror, and all this reminiscing and the special supper was because of that, because Margaret's way of escaping Coral's arrangements was going to be to cut her wrists in a hot bath. And she meant for May to go, too—that was the pillow, the coming down in the night and looking: she'd had it in her mind a long time, before Coral came. May shouted. "Pah!" You have no right!

Margaret stopped in midsentence.

May shouted, tears in her eyes, You have no right—leave me alone! I don't belong to you, you can't decide that for me! "Pocket damn! Boat pocket damn!"

"Oh, May—" Margaret's hand came toward her, and May pushed it hard away, sobbing. "Oh, May, what is it—oh—" Margaret said, her voice tight, pinched.

May struggled up on her pillows, grabbed one pillow clumsily from behind her and held it up to Margaret. "Boat damn!" she yelled.

She pushed her face into it, and then threw it to the floor. "Boat pocket damn damn!" Pointing to the stairs, to her own wrist, to Margaret. "Boat damn!"

"May—May, wait—listen, May—oh, what am I supposed to do? What would I do all alone, May? What would you do without me?"

I'd get along fine, May said. "Pocket." But she was growing calmer already, just because she knew, now, and she had made Margaret know that she did. Now Margaret would not be able to do it, not in cold blood, even if May were sound asleep. And now Margaret was crying.

"I don't know what else to do—you don't want to go to that place, you know you don't. Oh, May, I've tried to take good care of you—I remember when you were born, I remember the first time I saw you—I was only three, but I remember!"

This time May struggled, tried to catch how it began, how the something like memory came up so swift and sure, memory, though, of things she did not know, things she remembered but not with these events, and not a remembered story, either: imagining, she felt, I am imagining, but it was as strong as memory, as dream.

:The shade bumping gently against the window frame when she woke up from her nap, and she lay still, hearing that and listening to someone coming down the hall. Father came in, who had been plowing. Father said Mother was tired and must rest, Mother who had never been tired, and so she must get up now and go across the road to Gran to let Mother be quiet, and sleep there tonight, too, come along. She lay still because Mother always brought a damp flannel to wipe the sleep from her face and hands, and Father had not, and the sleep was a heavy soft thing. Come along, Father said again, and she did, but because the sleep was still on her everything was light and strange. Father held her dress for her to put her arms into the sleeves, and he buttoned her. Her pocket was heavy with May Flower, who napped in there while she napped on the bed. Past the buzzing

lilac hedge, she saw the road as if there were a darkness between it and her sight. When Father took her hand to cross the road, the sleep lifted away: she worried then that she had no nightie, and Gran always said the hornets wouldn't bother you if you didn't bother them.

Margaret, the old woman Margaret, sat weeping quietly, which was how May could believe that this dream was not death, and she willed the weeping Margaret away again, for a while yet.

:Gran on her kitchen porch, looking up over Father at the house where Mother rested, who was never tired. "Well," Gran said, "here we are."

"Yes," Father said.

Under their voices she felt for May Flower's cool round head and found with her thumb the smooth ridge of the doll's ear.

"If you need me," Gran said.

"Yes," Father said. "Be a good girl."

"You'll want supper," Gran said.

"No, thank you," Father said. "She'd put one on. I'll come over in the morning."

Gran's hand was bones inside soft thinness, and May Flower thumped against her thigh when she went up the steps to stand with Gran, and Father went back across the road. Gran said, "What do you think, Miss Margaret Alice? Shall we make a rhubarb pie?"

May let it stop for a moment, and looked at Margaret. That's you, May said. "Boat." Margaret sat trying to stop crying, the tissue balled up in her hand. That's you I'm remembering, all of it. I never had such a doll.

:At bedtime Gran opened the blue chest and brought out a new nightie for her, with blue thread roses on the collar, and she brushed Margaret's hair with the silver brush. "Tomorrow we'll go for a walk to the brook," she said. "Maybe the trilliums will be out. Do you know what your mother used to call trilliums? Stinking Benjamins." Gran laughed. "What a silly little girl your mother used to be. Hop into bed now."

In Gran's bed she had two pillows, one big and soft and the other with shiny binding.

"And maybe we'll be able to find some of last year's nuts and make some dishes for your dolly."

"You're right," Margaret said, the old Margaret, the weeping Margaret. "I can't, of course. But I only wanted to do the right thing—there isn't time, you know, she's got everything so *arranged*. But I'll call Mrs. Newhart. Yes."

:In that night Margaret was flung awake sweating in the bed with Gran and cried out a thin terror as she fought free of the sheet that had tangled around her, and then lay chilled in the unbroken sound of Gran's sleep, frightened to trembling because she could not tell whether her cry had made any sound for Gran to hear.

In the house across the road, assisted by huge Miss Benedict, Alice White was delivered of her second daughter, who cried out a thin triumph as she found the wide air, and then lay still on the boiled sheet and stared, feeling her skin for the first time, the cool dampness of it, the push and falling back of her chest.

"Boat," May breathed. I remember. Astonished, awed, the smell of it strong in her nose, the smell of Gran's bed, and the smell of herself briny with birth, and the smell of the boiled sheets.

"Actually," Margaret said, "I think if people knew, a great many would be willing to help us. I just mustn't let Coral push me that way."

"Hush," May said.

:After breakfast Margaret was ready to go for their walk, but Gran said they must wait a bit, until Father had come. She gave Margaret a basin of water and a towel and let her give May Flower a bath on the kitchen porch. Margaret whispered fervently to May Flower of the acorn cups, and took care not to get soap in her eyes, and if only she would be a good baby and not fuss along the way or be naughty while they hunted for the nuts. Then she dried her tenderly and

poured the water over the railing for the pinks. She held the doll then, sitting on the top step, pretending that the ticks she heard against the side of the house were not hornets but maple seed spinning; still, she started up and back in panic once at a dark swoop just outside her vision.

Father came with the smell of the barn and the milk house still on him, and Gran laughed as she poured his coffee. "So, Miss Margaret," Gran said. "What do you think of that?"

Margaret thought instead of the sound May Flower would make if she should wake and roll from where Margaret had left her and fall by accident into the pump organ in Gran's parlor.

"May," Father said. "May Ellen."

"After your mother," Gran nodded. "Very pretty. Don't you think that's a pretty name for your new little sister, Margaret?"

"Yes," Margaret said.

May Flower was still quite safe, but Margaret tucked her back into her pocket just the same, and Father stayed for dinner. When he left it was too late for their walk, they must have naps; perhaps tomorrow, because see how it looks like rain. That night there was thunder, and Margaret was afraid to sleep. Far into the dark she listened, and then Gran came in and undressed and came to bed. When Father came in the morning Margaret had wrapped May Flower deep in the new nightie so she wouldn't get chilled on the way home. She waited on the steps of the kitchen porch while Father and Gran talked and Father drank coffee. When he came out she stood up, and Gran was talking and Father laughed. Then he stopped and put his hand on Margaret's head. "Be a good girl, Margaret," he said. "Help your Gran, won't you?"

"Why, dear, whatever have you brought this out for? Oh, I see— well, we'll get your dolly a softer blanket than that. Come along," Gran said.

Far away in some house where Margaret had never been, Mother lay resting on a dim bed, and beside the bed sat a little girl in a chair like the one in a picture of Mother when she was a silly little girl in Gran's parlor.

"My, yes," Gran said, "and we've still got the dusting to do."

"May? You did say hush, didn't you?" Margaret's old fallen face flushed and excited. "You just said hush, and pocket—well!" She smiled. "I don't see how they can call that no progress, now can they?"

:By the day Father came and said to come along home and meet little May, the lilacs had gone brown and quiet. Margaret held Father's hand and went with him into the kitchen, cautious because this house was already strange to her, the furniture oddly sized, the smell rich with unfamiliar tones of food she hadn't eaten and washing done some new way. Mother was upstairs, Father said, and he too spoke quietly, as if they were visiting. The breeze came in around the quiet. Margaret followed through the parlor, where there was no sign of a new little girl, and then up the stairs.

"I think I'll just telephone Coral and tell her she'll have to make some other arrangements. Shall I?"

"No," May said. "No boat." She shook her head carefully, afraid, at the motion, that this strange memory might be another stroke, with the rushing noise and the sadness of it, afraid to do anything that would keep her from knowing the rest of it. Even if it was death, the dead coming to claim her, greet her, explain it all to her.

"No, I suppose not," Margaret said. And went slumped in her chair, so fast that May was frightened for a second, before Margaret began again to cry. "No, I don't suppose that would make any difference to her, not if you got up and walked. I don't suppose anything would make any difference—oh, May, I don't want to go! I'd rather be dead!"

:"Is that my big girl?" Mother called, who was simply Mother after all and sat in her regular dress in the bedroom rocker, so Margaret ran at last to climb as she knew how into Mother's lap and be rocked and feel Mother's laugh happy in her chest.

"See?" Mother said, and turned her face that Margaret had hardly seen. So Margaret's running and climbing stopped before it had become more than something like a stumble, and she looked into the bend of Mother's arm where Mother's face turned. The new little girl who was so quiet that she could come and stay when Mother was so tired and must rest disappeared forever: Margaret felt in her place come up like deep weariness the low rustle of breathing large and warm along her body, and a certainty of the nearness of something so profoundly sating that Margaret could never have known it by the name of milk or even breast, and a relaxation so complete it could ignore as if forever the texture and tension of what held it into possibility: Margaret knew, for a long loosening instant, loss. She saw the face of the baby asleep like the least and finest bit of a face almost lost in some drawing of a crowd in her storybook: nobody, and in full possession. Mother's voice was in it but the words of her voice did not mean: Margaret leaned over and against Mother's knees, reaching with neither hands nor eyes but only mouth for the simple small owner, to be herself in that utter bend of body and to have. She smelled its breath, raisin sweet and light, before her lips touched it. A child of three can swoon, and still miss her mark. Mother's arm came around (but not under, about, not that arm that cannot fail to provide the whole self rest) and Mother said, "See, Nick—how she loves her already!" And they told for years of Margaret loving her sister so, and called that hungry mouth reaching "kiss," and never knew Margaret's shock that the lips hers touched drew in and were as completely gone at the moment of capture as a brook minnow disappearing from the touch of a water-dipped finger, and with the same hinted and feeble anger at the disturbance, or that she would, if the lips had been there for her own, she would have sucked them, trying to take her place there on the arm of their mother.

"Of course she does," Father said. But he put his hand on Margaret's shoulder and pulled her gently back from May.

"I would—I'd rather be dead." Margaret's voice was calm now, calm and quiet, and the tears were all past. May looked at her, saw her, and saw too that child on Gran's porch, waiting. *I never knew,* May thought. *I never knew, and maybe this is not how it was.* Looking at Margaret. Who had meant murder. As rescue.

But May could not find any anger now. *I was born,* she thought. *Like that. I.* She shivered, knowing the cool air on that damp skin that had been hers. *And yours,* she thought, to Margaret, so quiet now.

"I think I'd better go up now," Margaret said. "I'll get your pill."

She went to the kitchen, and May was alone in the lamplight, as spent as if she'd been running and had just now stopped and caught her breath. The spaciousness she had felt earlier returned to her, but now it was not for a journey, not the feeling of being prepared to go, but something better, calmer. Some kind of arrival, instead. When Margaret came back in, her face set and closed, with the pill and the glass of water, May took her hand gently in her good hand. "Boat," she said. Meaning Remember, remember, Margaret: remember that little doll you had? Meaning Thank you for not wanting to leave me behind. You were kinder than I. Who did not mean to take your place by being born, you know that. Or by living, either, as I did. As we did.

Margaret said, "It's all right. Here's your pill."

May would not take it from her, not yet. "Pocket boat," she said. *You had named your doll the name they gave me.*

"You have your purse," Margaret said, her voice as dull as it had been when she was angry about Dutch.

So May took the pill from her but put it on the table beside the water glass, and said again, "Boat, boat," to keep her. She reached across herself for her purse and opened it.

Margaret was watching; her face was closed, but she was watching.

May pulled the handkerchief by the corners and spread it on the bed beside her. Six pills. She took the one Margaret had just brought and put it there too, and then, looking at Margaret to be sure she saw, she moved four of the pills into one pile and three into another.

May watched Margaret see, and watched her face soften as she understood, and watched her eyes come back to May's. "I'll be right back," she said, almost a murmur. She went to the kitchen and came back with the pill bottle, which she had never left carelessly where May could get it, and opened it and added the last five pills to the piles on May's handkerchief, so there were six each.

May let out her breath.

"They remind me of tea parties I used to make for my dolls," Margaret said softly. "With acorn cups and little leaves for plates. Gran used to help me get set up, I remember." May took Margaret's hand again, and turned it palm side up, and Margaret kept it like that while May moved the six pills carefully, clumsily, from the handkerchief to the hand. "I had a little tiny doll," Margaret said.

"Boat," May said, the last pill in Margaret's hand. With her hand she closed Margaret's fingers over them. Margaret's warm hand curled inside her own warm hand curled.

Margaret smiled. "All right," she said. "I'll just get a glass of water, May. And I'll tell you about that little doll. She used to fit in my pocket, I remember."